THE FIRST OF NINE

The Case of the Clementhorpe Killer

by

James Barrie

SEVERUS HOUSE
YORK, ENGLAND

'A cat is more intelligent than people believe,
and can be taught any crime.'
Mark Twain

Murder in Clementhorpe

Peter Morris was already dead when Theodore woke.

The dim hour before dawn was usually his favourite time of day. The birds are awake. Most cats are awake. Most people are asleep.

But this spring morning Theodore sensed something was not right. He blinked open his eyes and stretched.

His ears twitched.

The birds tweeted. The pigeons cooed. A young German shepherd whined. A car engine started up a few streets away. In the distance a train rumbled on its way to Leeds.

It sounded like any other morning. But why then did he feel something was not right?

He stirred from Emily's side. In the grey light he padded downstairs. He glanced at his food bowls. It would be at least an hour before they were filled. He exited through the cat flap, out into the yard.

He arched his back. He stretched out his paws. The hairs along his spine bristled.

A light breeze blew from the south. He tasted the damp morning air.

His own scent dominated the yard; he made sure of that. The potted herbs at the bottom the boundary wall he sprayed on a daily basis. He caught whiffs of other cats from adjoining 'shared' territories. He took in the fragrance from what flora grew in this urban environment, laced with the stench of human-generated waste that lay decomposing in rubbish bins and split bin liners. He made out the faint smell of cocoa hanging in the air.

1

He renewed his scent in a couple of locations before jumping up onto the boundary wall and making his way to the back wall.

He picked his way across the clematis, his ears twitching. He crossed the concrete plinth that spanned the back gate. He continued along the back walls, down the hill, until he was standing diagonally across from the house with the pigeon loft.

The house was on the corner of an access road to the back alley. The pigeon loft was fixed high up on the back gable wall. The yard was surrounded by a six foot high brick wall. On top of the wall was a wooden trellis, eighteen inches high. A single strand of rusted barbed wire was suspended two inches above the trellis.

Set into the wall was a wooden gate, coated black with thick creosote. The gate was never left open. Certainly not at this early hour, thought Theodore. But this morning the gate was open a few inches. Wide enough for a cat to slip through.

Theodore looked up and down the back alley, then jumped down from the wall. He padded over the grey hexagonal cobblestones. In front of the gate he paused and looked up and down the alley. He noticed a stocky black cat called Arthur at the crest of the hill. Arthur licked his paws in the long shadows, his back to Theodore.

Theodore turned back to the gate and, without further hesitation, padded into the yard.

The yard was all concrete, with leaves, feathers and other windblown debris gathered in the corners and against the bottom of the walls. Against the back wall lent a folded stepladder.

Theodore looked up at the pigeons perched on the eaves of the loft, cooing excitedly. He circled the yard. He looked up at the pigeons again. They cooed down at him: a provocation to Theodore. 'You can't get at us. You can't get at us,' they called, their napes glistening green and blue in the early morning sun.

Pea-brainers, Theodore thought, miaowing up at them with irritation.

Again he circled the yard, his tail straight up.

'You can't get at us,' the pigeons cooed down. 'You can't get at us.'

Just you wait…, thought Theodore.

The pigeon loft was of three-storey construction, with a pitched, felted roof. It measured about three foot by two and a half, taller than it was wide, and stood a foot proud of the red brick wall. Before that morning it had housed half a dozen birds.

Theodore turned and noticed the door to an outbuilding; it too was ajar. He approached and, in the shadows, made out a tartan slipper, its black shiny sole facing him. He went closer, and that was when he discovered the body.

Peter Morris lay on his front. He wore brown corduroy trousers and a blue checked shirt, the upper part dyed maroon with blood. A dark pool extended from what had been his head, now a colourful mess of shattered bone, congealed blood and grey brain. Pigeon feed had spilled from an upturned sack. The little seeds coated the dead man's head. It was more like some horrific dessert than a human head.

Theodore looked at the body with the same expression as he would a dead moth. He had never seen a dead human before. His instinct was to turn tail and head home.

He was shortly back on the bed he had left just minutes before. He stood on Emily's shoulder as she lay on her side. He pushed in his paws as hard as he could. He dabbed at her face with the pads of his paws.

She pushed him away with a heavy groan. 'It's too early,' she complained, her voice hoarse. 'I'm not feeding you yet.'

He pressed his paws into her shoulder again, this time applying his claws. She pushed him away again. But now she had her eyes open. She rolled onto her back and was met by Theodore's wide green stare. He stood on her chest purring noisily. She turned and glanced at the digital figures on her radio alarm clock.

'It's not even six o'clock,' she groaned. 'It's too early.'

She rolled back over, pulling the duvet around her shoulders so only her face was exposed. 'There's no way I'm going to start getting up this early just to feed you.'

Her voice was thick; she'd a bottle of Pinot Grigio to herself the night before.

Theodore jumped down and a minute later he was back in the Morris's yard. He ran to a corner, collected several grey feathers in his mouth and returned to Emily's side. He dropped the dirty grey feathers onto her face.

She spluttered, swiping the feathers away with her hand.

'What the!' she said, rubbing at her face before sitting up.

Her eyes opened wide as she examined the dirty feathers that lay on the bed sheet.

'Fiddlesticks! You've only gone and eaten one of his pigeons.'

Theodore jumped down from the bed. He made for the top of the stairs and paused, his tail held upright, making sure Emily was following before he went down. He didn't have to wait long. He soon heard her feet on the bare boards of the bedroom floor. He dashed down the stairs and through the dining room. He paused in the kitchen until he was sure she had reached the bottom of the stairs, then exited into the yard, the cat flap snapping shut behind him.

Emily grabbed her black woollen coat from the coat stand and pulled on her slippers before unlocking the backdoor.

She spotted Theodore standing on the back wall of the yard. 'Get back here now,' she called.

Theodore padded across the clematis, crossed the concrete plinth and jumped down into the alley, disappearing from sight.

'For heaven's sake!' Emily said, walking over to the back gate and doing up the two middle buttons of her coat as she went.

She unbolted the gate and entered the alley. In the grey light she saw Theodore approach the house with the pigeon loft.

'Get out of there,' she hissed.

But Theodore had already disappeared inside the yard.

She glanced up and down the back alley, did up another button on her coat, and then walked down the hill. She pushed the black gate open and entered the yard.

Theodore was standing in front of an outbuilding. A handful of pigeons took to the air and fluttered overhead, beating their grey wings.

She walked over and picked Theodore up with both hands and held him to her chest. Theodore let his body go limp. Then she saw the body. Theodore was dropped to the ground.

Her scream was heard by over a hundred people, many dragged from their dreams by the shrill screech.

At that moment the bells of St Clement's at the bottom of the hill began to clang out six o'clock. They were shortly followed by the bells of York Minster, just over a mile away.

The next person to arrive at the murder scene was Michael Butler, whose house backed onto the Morris's.

He entered the yard, dressed in tight running gear, saw Emily and approached the shed. At that moment the back door of the house swung open and the very recently widowed Wendy Morris marched out, tying the cord of her mauve towel dressing gown as she approached.

'What's going on out here?' she demanded.

Emily opened her mouth to speak but no words came out.

'It appears that Mr Morris has had an accident,' Michael said, standing in front of the outbuilding.

'An accident?' Wendy said. 'Let me see.' She approached the outbuilding but Michael stood in her way.

'You shouldn't look in there,' Michael said. 'I think he's dead.'

'Don't tell me what I can and can't do in my own yard,' Wendy said.

She pushed past him. 'Peter!' she cried, dropping to her knees. 'Oh, Peter...

Emily started crying.

'He's dead,' Wendy said, still stooping over the body of her husband.

'I'd better go and call the police,' Michael said.

He hurried out of the yard.

Wendy backed out of the outbuilding. She turned and faced Emily. 'How did you get in?'

She pointed her forefinger at Emily's chest.

'Through the gate,' Emily said, sniffing. She wiped her nose on the sleeve of her coat, leaving a silvery trail behind. 'It was open…'

'He never leaves the gate open.'

'It was open this morning,' she blubbered. 'My cat…'

Emily began to cry in earnest.

'Your cat?' Wendy asked. 'What's your cat got to do with this?'

Emily looked around for Theodore to corroborate her story but he was nowhere to be seen.

'My cat,' she said, shaking her head. 'He brought some feathers into my house. I thought…'

'You thought what?'

Wendy marched to the back of the yard. Several pigeons had settled up on the eaves of the slate-tiled roof. A further two fluttered overhead. 'One of his pigeons is missing,' she said. 'Ethel...'

Emily stared at her through red rimmed eyes. 'Ethel?'

'Yes, Ethel...' Wendy said. 'I bet your cat's had it.'

She looked at the door of the outbuilding, where her dead husband lay. She looked at her hands, smudged red with blood. She looked at the open gate.

'Peter would never have left that gate open,' she went on. 'Someone's murdered him and your cat has made off with one of his birds.'

She put her hands on her hips.

Then Michael strode back into the yard. He was followed by his partner, Philip Sutcliffe, dressed in purple silk pyjamas.

'The police are on their way,' Michael said.

Then, as if on cue, they heard the siren of a police car as it made its way from Fulford, on the other side of the River Ouse.

'What's happened?' Philip asked, wiping sleep from an eye.

He crossed the yard to the outbuilding and peered in. The police siren grew louder. 'Ugh,' he said, grimacing. 'That's not very nice.'

Wendy pushed her hands into the pockets of her dressing gown, her fists clenched. 'Somebody's killed him,' she said. 'And her cat has had Ethel.'

'Ethel?' Philip asked.

'Yes, Ethel. She was one of his pigeons.'

Emily whimpered something incomprehensible and began crying again.

Then there was a loud knocking at the front door.

'I'll go and let them in,' Michael said.

'I can get it,' Wendy said. She turned and marched back inside.

From behind the wooden trellis that topped the back wall, Theodore noticed that she was wearing slippers, large fur-lined slippers.

He hadn't eaten any pigeon. He didn't even know what one tasted like. Now I'm accused of killing one, he thought, looking up at the remaining birds.

He would prove them wrong. He would find out who or what had taken the pigeon. He would clear his name and, in doing so, find out who had killed Peter Morris too.

In the distance he heard more sirens approaching. Two police officers were standing in front of the outbuilding. Wendy Morris, arms folded across her bosom, stood behind the police officers. Michael and Philip had retreated to the gate. Michael lifted his feet in turn and glanced at the soles of his running shoes. Probably checking he hasn't stood in any blood, thought Theodore.

Emily was standing near the back wall, unaware that Theodore was only a few yards from her head.

Her eyes were red rimmed from crying. Her hair was a tangled mess of strawberry blonde. Her black woollen coat ended mid-thigh, below which her baggy pink pyjama bottoms showed. On her feet she wore her old Garfield slippers. The ridiculous orange lasagne-loving cats looking a little worse for wear.

Not quite the Watson I had in mind, Theodore thought, blinking in the early morning sun.

The Significance of the Blue Cobblestone

Theodore had been whimsically named after a chubby rodent from an animated film. He was more fortunate, however, than some of his feline contemporaries. Mr Bo Jangles, Prissy Paws and Fluffy McWuffy Pants were just a few of the embarrassing names that the more unfortunate Clementhorpe cats had to carry. It was hardly any wonder that they rarely answered their owners' calls.

He had been bred by Jennifer, a spindly spinster living in a bungalow on the outskirts of Malton. Her cats numbered up to forty at a time, depending on how many she could part with. She fed her 'children' Royal Canin biscuits and raw chicken drumsticks, while she subsisted on a diet of porridge and toast.

Theodore had spent the first months of his life shut up in a cage along with his siblings in the spare bedroom. The other kittens were content to sleep, eat and play, but Theodore wanted out. And as he grew the feelings of needing to escape increased.

The day Jennifer brought the kittens out to show Emily, he could stand it no more. As soon as the cage door was opened, he pushed his siblings aside and flung himself out. He forward rolled across the living room carpet and then circled the room frantically, looking for a way out.

Jennifer's mouth dropped.

'He's adorable,' Emily said, picking him up.

'He's certainly a lively one,' Jennifer said.

'Can I take him home today?'

Theodore's father was a Scottish Fold, his mother a Ragdoll. He hadn't inherited the folded ears of his father, but like his father his long silvery grey fur was streaked with charcoal. His chest and underside were snow white, his emerald green eyes were underscored with white mascara, and his nose was the colour of cooked liver.

Around his neck he wore a purple velvet collar, and attached to the collar was a small silver disc bearing his name and Emily's mobile phone number.

'He's too pretty to be a boy,' said Michael.

Emily looked out of the window to see her cat sitting on the back wall staring across at her. 'What are you doing there?' she said.

Theodore widened his eyes, as if to say, 'What are *you* doing there?'

'Does he sit there often?' Emily asked.

'Sometimes,' Michael replied. 'He's an inquisitive one.'

'You can say that again,' Emily said, thinking of the events of that morning.

'He sometimes watches me while I'm working…' Michael said.

'He gets around, I guess,' said Emily.

'I don't let him in,' Michael went on. 'I'm allergic to cats.' He got up. 'I'll go and get the tea.'

Emily, Michael and Philip had been taken to Fulford Police Station that morning to make statements. Having made her way home, she'd decided to call on Michael. She hadn't spoken to him much before, but she felt the need to talk about what had happened to someone, and not knowing anyone else on the street had called on Michael.

While he was in the kitchen making tea, Emily glanced around the room. There were several framed pencil drawings hanging on the wall, over a purple clad chaise longue. The pictures were all York street scenes – Stonegate, Goodramgate, Micklegate… But they were all curiously devoid of people.

Maybe he can't draw people, Emily thought.

There was a sheet of paper pinned onto a drawing board at the back of the room. An anglepoise lamp lit up the white rectangle of paper. She could make out some faint pencil marks. Drawing equipment was laid out on a table beside the drawing board. Not a pencil out of place. Also on the table, there was a little wooden mallet, the sort used to tenderize steaks.

I wonder what that's doing there, she thought.

From the back wall of Michael's house Theodore also wondered what the mallet was for.

Emily didn't know much about Michael. He was already living on Avondale Terrace when she'd moved in two years ago. He sometimes wore thick-rimmed tortoiseshell glasses, other times he must wear contact lenses, she thought.

Philip had only appeared recently. She wasn't sure if he lived with Michael, or just stayed over some nights.

She'd learned that Philip had had to go to work. He worked shifts at a fried chicken shop in the city centre. 'McChicko's', Michael had called it.

'Did you know Peter Morris at all?' she asked Michael, when he returned. He was carrying a tray with a tea pot and two cups, all matching porcelain.

'Not really,' he said, putting the tea things down and arranging them on the table. 'I used to hear him on a night. He talked to his pigeons.'

'Really?'

'Yes. That's not so surprising, is it? I bet you talk to your cat.'

'Yes, but that's different,' Emily said, biting on her bottom lip. 'I mean Theodore is intelligent.'

Michael shrugged. 'Well, he used to talk to them... He had names for them too. Deirdre, Lily, Daisy, Ethel... I think Ethel must have been his favourite. "Oh, Ethel," he used to say, "You are a beauty..." Late at night when I was lying in bed I could hear him... I sleep with the window open... Didn't you ever hear him?'

'No. Never... I go to sleep with the radio on,' Emily said. 'And I live further up the hill.'

They were both quiet for a minute.

Emily sipped at her tea. It was slightly citrusy. 'What do you think she's going to do with the pigeons?' she said.

'Probably sell them. The police said to me that some of them may be worth a bit. Maybe whoever killed Peter did it over a pigeon.'

'Over a pigeon?' Emily said. 'I don't believe that.'

'Well, it would clear your cat – if someone had stolen the bird.'

On the back wall, Theodore pricked up his ears.

'Whoever killed Peter Morris had to have a reason,' Michael went on. 'A motive if you like... If someone had found out that those birds of his were worth a lot of money...'

'They might have broken into his yard to steal his birds,' Emily continued the chain of thought.

'And Peter surprised them...'

'And they hit him over the head...' Emily said. 'And killed him.'

'No,' Michael said, shaking his head.

'No?' Emily said.

Michael took a sip of tea. 'They're not connected,' he said. 'The murder and the missing pigeon... It was probably your cat that killed it.'

'But you said...'

'The murder is unrelated to the pigeon. Someone bumped off the old man and then your cat made off with one of his birds.'

'He wouldn't have done,' Emily said, glancing out of the window and meeting Theodore's stare.

'He's a cat, isn't he? Cats kill birds... It's nature. And didn't you say he dropped pigeon feathers on your bed? There's the evidence. He as good as owned up to it.'

'That doesn't mean he killed the pigeon. He just wanted to get my attention. He discovered the body and he came to get me.'

'I think you are giving him more credit than he's worth.'

Emily sighed and shook her head.

'What's done is done,' Michael said, matter of factly. 'Even if your cat killed his pigeon, what's the big deal? It's only a bird at the end of the day. A rat with wings at that.'

He placed his teacup back in its saucer. 'A rat with wings,' he repeated. He had his right leg over the left and was jigging it up and down.

Emily stared down at his agitated leg, and noticing Michael said, 'I didn't have my run today…'

Evidently Michael was not a friend of either the feathered or the furry among us, thought Theodore. He turned and looked at the pigeon loft on the gable wall. Now Ethel was gone, there were five pigeons; the day before there had been half a dozen.

He watched as a police officer cycled down the hill. She didn't notice Theodore on the wall. She was looking the other way. Towards Wendy Morris's house.

Theodore jumped down into the alley and up onto the other side, on top of Wendy's back wall.

The trellis had square openings, about two inches apart. Theodore peered through the trellis and spotted Wendy, sitting at her kitchen table, her back to the window. Dirty dishes soaked in the sink. The knuckle of a rolling pin stood proud of the greyish brown washing up water. An early evening soap opera was on. A small television tucked into the corner. An advertisement break interrupted the programme.

'All this baking!' Irene said. 'I don't know how you can eat with what's happened… Poor Peter. I mean he had plenty more life in him, didn't he?'

'I can always freeze them,' Wendy said.

'What's that?'

'I'll freeze the pies. Unless you'd like to take one. I've not got that much room in my freezer come to think of it.'

'Go on then,' Irene said. 'I don't mind if I do. If I don't eat it, Rocky will.'

'Best to keep busy,' Wendy said. 'That's what they say.'

'And they haven't found the murder weapon? I doubt they will now. I mean it could have been owt. A sledgehammer. A brick. A lump of concrete. I'll bet it's at the bottom of the Ouse by now. No doubt they'll be out searching people's backyards tomorrow morning. I doubt they will find owt though.'

'Emmerdale's back on,' Wendy said, nodding her head at the television in the corner.

'Oh, so it is.'

The two old ladies turned to face the television. However, Wendy did not follow the plot as it played out on the small screen. Instead the scenes from her own day replayed themselves in her head.

She thought of that scream that had got her from her bed. Then the silly girl sobbing in her yard; the man in tight running gear dashing off to call the police; his friend in purple pyjamas. Then the police arriving.

They took away the two men and the girl to Fulford Police Station, and then she was also taken to make a statement. When she returned from Fulford several hours later Peter had gone and the shed floor had been scrubbed clean. Two young female officers had sat with her into the evening, asking questions. Wendy was not sure if she were being counselled or questioned.

She was told by the quietly spoken police officer, her hand on hers, that her husband had died instantly and would have felt no pain. Then the other asked quite bluntly if she had any idea what might have done such damage. Wendy said that she didn't know.

'He wouldn't have known what hit him,' the first officer said.

The young police woman asked her if she had anywhere else to spend the night. 'A relation you could stay with?' she suggested. 'It may be an idea after what's happened...'

Wendy shook her head. 'I'll stay here,' she said. 'I have a friend who'll come and sit with me... Irene.'

As evening set in, Theodore knew that the police investigation would be put on hold until the next day. Now his own investigation could begin.

Night-time was a friend to the cat. While humans can only see darkness, a cat can pick out a thousand shades of grey. He walked along the back walls, inspecting the backyards and gardens, looking for anything out of place. Unlike the police, he didn't need to seek permission to enter a person's yard.

There was a much neglected garden to the rear of No. 19, the house next door to his own. The grass had not been cut in years. Every curtain in the house was closed. They were never opened as far as Theodore could tell. It began to spit with rain but Theodore did not feel it through his thick coat.

He jumped down into the overgrown rectangle of lawn. He had explored this garden numerous times in recent months. In among the long, wet undergrowth were crumpled beer cans, plastic bottles, crisp packets, sodden newspapers, a bicycle wheel, the remains of a takeaway tied up in a plastic bag and numerous little blue plastic bags of canine excrement.

Theodore sensed something foreign among the undergrowth, something that hadn't been there before and had no right being there now.

He approached through the long wet grass, his head close to the ground, sniffing the air. In front of him there lay a hexagonal-shaped cobblestone, just like the ones that paved the back alley. Its glazed blue surface was splashed with dried blood.

He thought back to the conversation he had overheard between Wendy and her neighbour Irene: 'A sledgehammer. A brick. A lump of concrete...'

It was still raining; the raindrops splashed the surface of the cobblestone – washing away the blood. Washing away the evidence.

Theodore stood staring at the cobblestone lying in the overgrown grass, his tail held aloft. He looked at the boundary wall that separated this garden from his own yard. There was no way he could transport the cobblestone to his own house, to Emily. His only hope was to transport Emily to the cobblestone.

She was lying on the sofa in the front room, the television on, a glass of wine on the little round table in front of her. She was watching a cookery programme.

Theodore miaowed loudly from the doorway.

'Come here, Theo,' she said, her voice tired.

Theodore jumped up by her side and allowed her to hug him to her. He began to purr.

'Ugh. You're all wet.'

Theodore jumped down and walked to the door, wagging his tail from side to side.

He miaowed as loudly as he could. He turned round to see Emily still watching television.

'You've got food,' she said and took a sip of wine.

Theodore paced the hallway.

He remembered what Irene had said: 'No doubt they'll be out searching people's backyards tomorrow morning.'

He heard the rain patter at the windows. The blood will be washed away by the morning, he thought. Even if they discovered the cobblestone, they would not realize its significance.

He stared up at Emily and miaowed once more. Emily shook her head. 'I can't do anything about the rain,' she said.

She took her mobile phone from the arm of the sofa and began to tap the screen.

At times like these Theodore felt complete exasperation at his inability to be understood by his human. Like a driver beeping his horn and flashing his lights, trying to warn oncoming traffic of a collapsed bridge on the road ahead, Theodore could resort only to miaowing, purring or hissing in order to communicate. How was he going to alert the authorities to the significance of the blue cobblestone?

He thought for a minute, raised his tail, and then headed back outside.

Emily woke in the middle of the night and knew that Theodore was not in his usual spot: the pillow beside her own. The radio talked quietly on her bedside table. Minster FM informed her that: 'following the murder of a pensioner in the Clementhorpe area of York, the police are now looking for someone wearing pink pyjamas and gloves.'

They should put on some more sensible clothes, thought Emily, still half asleep.

She reached over and turned the radio off. She turned on her bedside lamp. She looked at the empty pillow by her side. Then she got up and went downstairs, calling her cat's name. He wasn't in the house.

Had something happened to Theodore now?

She grabbed her coat, pulled on her Garfield slippers and unlocked the back door. Outside it was still raining. She called his name quietly and a minute later heard a soft thud as he landed in the corner of the yard. He ran towards her.

'Theodore, come here. What on earth have you been up to?' She scooped him up.

'Oh my God. You're soaking. Look at the state of you.'

Theodore's fur was sodden; twigs and other organic debris entwined in his fur.

Emily carried him upstairs to the bathroom. She towelled him dry and put him to bed on a fresh towel on his pillow. He was soon asleep.

The Strange Fish at No.19

Avondale Terrace is located in the Clementhorpe district of York, a short walk from the city centre. It lies to the south of the City Walls. The River Ouse and Rowntree Park are to the west; the residential sprawl of South Bank to the south, and the Knavesmire and the racecourse to the west. It is now a popular residential area. It used to be populated by railway and chocolate factory workers. These days the newcomers, living side by side with the old timers, are young professionals, mostly without children, who commute to jobs in Leeds, as York has little industry of its own except for tourism.

The Clementhorpe streets are formed by rows of Victorian terraced housing, fronting onto the car-lined streets and backing onto narrow alleys. The alleys are paved with hexagonal cobbles, and across the wet cobbles of the back alley between Avondale and Alcuin Terraces two police officers descended the gentle hill. They were not dressed in pink pyjamas and gloves, but were wearing their uniforms.

They peered over walls into the backyards and little courtyard gardens, not expecting to find anything of any significance but enjoying being out in the early morning sunshine that had followed the rain.

At a quarter to eight, one police officer turned to the other and said, 'Well, have a look at that.'

His colleague peered over the wall. It was just an overgrown little garden with rubbish strewn around. At first he did not see what had caught his colleague's attention. But then he saw it too.

The long grass had been pushed down in a long line extending from the back wall. At the end of the line was a circular clearing, where the grass had been flattened, and in the middle of the clearing there was a blue hexagonal cobblestone.

'I think we'd better get forensics over,' the policeman said, reaching for his radio.

His colleague added, 'And we'd better have a little chat with whoever lives here.'

The house belonged to Craig Foster, a middle-aged man with unruly ginger hair, which extended down the sides of his freckled face.

When questioned over his whereabouts the night Peter Morris had been killed, Craig did not have an alibi as such.

He had been home alone that evening. When asked what he'd watched on television, he admitted to not owning a television. When asked what he had been doing, he said that he had been up in his attic room looking at the stars through his telescope. Oblivious to time, he was not sure when he had gone to bed. He claimed not to know anything of the murder even though it was already all over the local news and on the tips of everyone's tongues.

As he was being helped into the back of a police van, Theodore heard Craig reiterate to the police officer that he had been staring at the stars from his attic room the whole evening, adding with a stammer that he was a keen astrologist.

Theodore furrowed his brow. If Craig was so keen on the study of the stars, why would he confuse astronomy with the party games of astrology?

He was lying. He was the murderer without doubt.

He had assisted the police in getting the killer. Now he just needed to find out what had happened to Ethel the pigeon.

Within a couple of hours, a white tent had been erected over the back garden of No. 19, under which several police officers were on their hands and knees conducting a fingertip search.

Theodore looked down at the grey shadows dancing beneath the canvas from the back bedroom window and yawned with satisfaction at his handiwork. He gave himself a lick over and went down to have a light lunch of mashed cod fillets that Emily had left out. He returned to bed, satisfied that the police could now be left to progress the investigation while he caught up on his sleep.

The officer who had spotted the cobble in the rear garden of No. 19 returned to the police station to submit his report, in which he included the fact that the grass around the cobble had been flattened down. If this had not been the case, the cobble would probably have remained in the long grass and its significance would never have been realized. Neither he nor any of his colleagues could offer an explanation. A senior officer muttered something about 'believing in crop circles next', and the matter was dropped. It would therefore never be acknowledged that the police had had a little feline assistance in discovering what would soon transpire to be the murder weapon.

Forensics detected small amounts of blood on the cobble despite the heavy rain the night following the murder. It did not take them long to confirm that the blood had belonged to the late Peter Morris. However, if there had been any fingerprints, they had been washed away. Or the murderer had worn gloves.

The police began a thorough search of the inside of No.19 while Craig was detained at Fulford. In the attic room they found his telescope and a computer. The rest of the house was untidy and cluttered with stacks of magazines, newspapers, equipment and furniture that had suffered from long years of neglect. One of the bedrooms the police had difficulty in entering: it was so crammed with boxes.

It would take a team of twelve officers some time to go through the house and its contents.

Shortly after midday a police officer visited Wendy.

'He used that cobble to keep the shed door open,' she told the police officer. 'I realized it was gone when I went to feed his birds last night. The door swung shut on me.'

The police officer scribbled into her notepad and took a sip of tea. On arriving she had insisted on making a cup for both her and Wendy, although Wendy had protested.

Wendy wondered what she was writing into her pad.

She sipped at her tea. It was too weak. Wendy liked the tea bag left in. 'I was going to tell you about that cobble today,' she told the police officer. 'Is it important?'

'You could say that. They detected Mr Morris's blood on it.'

'You think whoever did it used that cobble?'

'The police are questioning the resident of No. 19 Avondale Terrace… The fact that the cobblestone was found in his garden doesn't mean that he did it. It's more than likely that whoever did it, threw it over the wall as they left the scene.'

'I heard he's a strange fish,' Wendy said. 'Lives by himself and never opens his curtains. He wears one of those army coats. Though I doubt he's ever served a day in his life.'

'He's being questioned at present, Mrs Morris.'

'Call me Wendy. Less of this Mrs Morris.'

The police officer took a sip of her tea. 'So you didn't hear anything the night before last?'

'No. I sleep like a log. I've already told them that.'

'And what about Mr Morris? When did he go to bed?'

'He goes to bed early… Went to bed early, I mean. Always up with the birds, he was. But I like to stay up and watch the telly.'

'We've had more than one person say they heard raised voices in the night. A man and a woman, perhaps? You didn't hear anything?'

'The first I knew something was up was when that girl screamed... A man and a woman, you say?'

'We've had differing reports. Different people heard different things. It's quite usual.'

They sipped at their mugs of tea.

'They meant the world to him those birds,' Wendy said. 'He used to show them. Ethel won best in show at Pickering last year. He got his photo in his magazine. Ever so proud he was.'

She got up and went into the front room. The curtains had not been opened since the night Peter had been murdered, and wouldn't be opened again until he was in the ground.

A minute later she returned with a yellowed magazine. She opened it to an array of faded photographs.

'That's Peter,' she said, pointing her finger at a photograph.

Peter Morris cradled Ethel to his chest with one hand, a rosette held in the other. He smiled at the camera. He had pointed features with protruding eyebrows. He was bald on top and the hair at the sides of his head was silver. He stooped slightly like tall men sometimes do.

'He was a handsome man,' the police officer said.

Wendy swept a tear from her cheek with her forefinger. She wiped her hand on the front of her apron.

'I am sorry,' the police officer said.

'Sorry isn't going to bring him back.'

The police woman shook her head.

'I keep expecting him to come through that door,' Wendy said.

She stood up and went over to the kitchen sink, the half-drunk mug of weak tea in her hand. She poured the tea down the side of the bowl and looked out of the window. Through the trellis, she glimpsed a silver grey outline. 'It's that silly girl's cat,' she said. 'Returned to the scene of the crime. They do that, don't they?'

'What's that?'

'The criminal. They return to the scene of the crime, don't they?'

'I don't follow.'

The police officer stood up.

'The pigeon that went missing,' Wendy said. 'I reckon it was that cat that had it…'

The police officer approached the window but Theodore had already jumped down. 'Our priority is to find out who killed your husband.'

'Peter was paranoid about cats,' Wendy said. 'Paranoid that one would get at his birds. That's why he put the barbed wire on top of the fence and installed the lighting. He had it set so that even if a cat jumped on the wall, it'd come on…

'If owt got into the yard, he'd be out there in a flash.'

'So if someone had got in, the light would have come on and Peter would have gone down to investigate?'

'That's what I said.'

The police officer scribbled again in her pad.

Wendy was sure that she had already said all of this just yesterday but to a different police officer.

As Theodore made his way home in the late afternoon, something nagged at his mind. 'It's more than likely that whoever did it, threw the cobblestone over the wall as they left the scene,' the police officer had said. Theodore pondered the police officer's assertion and could not fault it. Whoever had killed Peter Morris had thrown the bloody cobble over the back wall of No. 19.

Would Craig have left the cobblestone in his own back yard?

It was possible but now seemed unlikely.

But if Craig wasn't the killer, who *had* murdered Mr Morris? What had happened to Ethel the missing pigeon? Was there in fact a link between the missing bird and the dead pensioner?

And, more importantly – had Emily filled his food bowls?

The Missing Birman Cat

Emily was not yet home. Theodore stared for some minutes at his empty food bowls. Then he went into the front room and lay in the bay window, on the folded woollen blanket that covered the wooden chest. The chest contained board games that were never played but Theodore didn't know that. He closed his eyes and soon fell asleep.

Like most cats he slept two thirds of the day, although he usually kept one ear open to the outside world. If humans would only sleep more, Theodore reflected, crime could be drastically reduced. Half the waking hours would surely mean half the crime.

Most days Emily left the television on to keep Theodore company. He tended to doze through many of the daytime offerings, but somehow absorbed an amazing amount of information. Theodore considered himself an expert on bargain hunting, overseas property acquisition and human relationship counselling. However, he preferred the crime dramas that were shown in the afternoons. His favourite was *Columbo*. He loved the cigar-toting, dishevelled homicide detective.

When he heard Emily parking her car up the street, he got to his paws and stretched.

Theodore knew all the cars on the street by their distinctive defects: the staccato from holes in exhausts, the groaning of engines that demanded tuning, the squeal of worn out brake pads. But he always recognized Emily's Volkswagen Beetle as she approached by the music playing from inside. She always had one of two albums playing in the cassette player.

One cassette was Michael Jackson's *BAD*; the other Leonard Cohen's *Greatest Hits*. She had bought the Michael Jackson at least ten years ago. The Leonard Cohen had been lent by an ex-boyfriend; she couldn't remember which. Depending on her mood, as she drove to and from work, she usually had one of the albums playing. Her aerial had been snapped off a couple of years earlier, and unable to buy cassettes any longer, the car was limited to the two albums or silence.

That evening, Theodore recognized the throaty voice of Cohen and knew she had not had the best of days. He was at the front door as she unlocked it.

She picked him and pushed her face into his chest, holding him there a full minute while he purred.

'I missed you, Theo,' she said, emerging from his fur.

Emily Blenkin had been in two minds that morning whether to go to work or not. She had a good excuse not to go after all. It's not every day your neighbour is battered to death. But then she'd decided it might take her mind off it.

She was acting manager of a furniture store at Monks Cross, a retail park on the other side of York, a tedious forty-five minute commute halfway around the ring road.

The store sold over-priced furniture and soft furnishings to the local well-to-do with money to fritter away on these luxury items. The customers were demanding and most of their demands unreasonable.

That morning she'd had to deal with an irate woman who had wanted to return a throw she had been using as a table cloth – after she had spilled red wine on it. Then, in the afternoon, there had been the rude young woman who had had a bookcase delivered which did not fit into her chosen recess. This was followed by a whiny woman who wanted to return a set of cushions that attracted dog hair. The cushions were indeed covered with fine golden hair and coated with what Emily hoped was dog drool and not anything worse.

She had wanted to tell them that she didn't care, that one of her neighbours had been murdered, and their petty concerns were just that. Petty.

But she hadn't. Instead she'd bitten the inside of her bottom lip until it was swollen and appeased the customers in accordance with the manual that they had to follow. Then she had sat in the stop-start traffic of the ring road at rush hour to get home.

She slumped down on the sofa and threw her coat across onto the other sofa. The LED on her telephone was blinking and she knew her mother had called; she always called when she knew Emily was at work. Emily reached over and played the telephone message.

'It's so awful,' Emily's mother said. 'To think you've been living next door to a murderer. Let's hope they *have* got him. If they haven't, that means there is some homicidal maniac still on the loose... I don't know how you can sleep at night...'

Her mother went on for several minutes, before finally declaring: 'Your father wants to say hello.'

'Hello,' her father said, and the message ended with an abrupt beep.

Emily paced the rooms of her house, Theodore at her heels. She walked past the empty food bowls several times but didn't notice their lack of contents.

She went into the yard and made sure that the gate was bolted. When she went back inside, she locked the door behind her. She opened a cupboard and removed the largest pan. She placed it on the kitchen side by the back door.

She returned to the lounge and picked up a leaflet that had been dropped through her front door a few days before. It was the menu from a local Chinese takeaway. The front of the leaflet had a cartoon picture of two little Chinese girls with pigtails and wide horizontal smiles.

She scanned the list of numbered meals, then took her mobile phone and dialled the takeaway. She ordered salt and pepper chicken wings, char sui pork, crispy noodles, egg foo yung and prawn crackers. When Emily was worried or upset, she ate. She was told it would be twenty minutes. She looked at her watch but didn't take in the time.

She went to the kitchen and retrieved a half bottle of white wine and a glass. Returning to the living room, she flicked on the television. She took her laptop from the table and put it on her lap.

Theodore jumped up beside her, rubbing his face against her thigh, nudging the laptop at the same time.

She still hadn't fed him. He purred loudly to remind her, and Emily stroked him behind the ears in return. He pushed his head against the side of the whirring laptop.

'Hey!' Emily said, pushing him away. 'Can't I just check my mail?'

Theodore maintained his offensive against the laptop until he was interrupted by a knock at the front door.

Emily put the laptop aside. She looked at her watch. It couldn't have been more than a few minutes since she'd called the takeaway, could it? She opened the door.

'Hello there,' a young man said in an overly-friendly voice. 'I'm from *The Press*. Would it be all right if I ask you a few questions about what happened the other morning? I understand you discovered the body... First on the scene, as they say…'

Emily looked at the man's blue checked shirt and grinning pink face through the gap in the door. From behind her Theodore miaowed.

'I really don't want to talk to anybody right now,' she said. 'I've just got in from work.'

'It will only take a minute… if you let me come in.'

The man stepped forward. Theodore miaowed once more.

'My cat,' Emily said, 'I don't like him getting out the front.'

She shut the door on the reporter, feeling a little mean as she did so. She understood that he was only doing his job.

Turning round, she said, 'Were you being protective of me, Theo?'

I think you might have forgotten to feed me, Theodore thought back.

She bent down and stroked him, saying, 'You're right, Theo. You just don't know who to trust these days.'

She then followed Theodore's raised tail into the kitchen.

Later that evening, as she was eating chicken wings from a silver foil carton that had taken almost an hour to arrive, she looked at the local newspaper website. The top story was the Clementhorpe murder. 'Suspect Detained,' the headline said.

There was a photograph of a man with ginger hair and side burns, getting into the back of a police van. Her next-door neighbour. Her mother had been right.

She saw him some mornings as she left for work, although he had never spoken to her. He seemed harmless enough, she thought. But you never can tell.

As she scrolled down the story, she soon discovered that he was called Craig Foster, worked at York Science Park, and had lived alone since his mother had passed away ten years ago. The brief description shouted 'Loner!'

'To think he lives just beyond that wall,' Emily said to Theodore. 'Thank goodness the police have got him so quickly.'

Let's hope that's the case, Theodore thought.

The story went on to mention that one of Peter Morris's pigeons was missing, suggesting that the pigeon could be worth as much as £15,000. It ended by stating that the bird had not been recovered. The story was sequenced to suggest that Peter Morris had been killed over the valuable pigeon. People had been murdered for much less, Emily thought.

Theodore stared at the ten inch screen as she scrolled down the story. There was a photograph of Peter Morris taken with one of his birds.

He had always said 'How do,' to Emily with a smile when she'd seen him in the back alley. Her eyes welled up. What had he ever done to hurt anybody? She cried for some minutes, felt a little better, and then finished her chicken wings.

She went to wash her hands and when she returned she discovered that Theodore had settled where she'd been sitting. She stroked his forehead and he purred in return. She sat down on the adjacent seat.

She signed onto her dating website and glanced at the messages that men she didn't know had sent her. There were twenty three. Not a bad day, she thought.

Five of these were from people living at least fifty miles away, including a couple from remote corners of Britain: towns or cities that Emily didn't even recognize the names of. She deleted these ones straight away. She then deleted those from people who did not even have a profile picture: married or ugly, she thought. Then went the beardies and baldies.

She scrolled through the remaining messages, deleting those she understood to be generic messages that could be sent out to twenty or a hundred prospective candidates at a time. She was left with five messages. She flicked through the accompanying profiles, deleting those she just didn't like the look of, or those profiles that included any reference to sports. Her ex had dominated the television with his Sky Sports.

She was left with one profile.

He listed as his likes red wine, pepperoni pizzas, Scrabble, several television programmes, then a list of music bands – many of which she hadn't heard of. She hoped he was joking about the Scrabble. She read on. He was a geologist. He had just a couple of photographs.

He was tall and slim with blue eyes, medium length dark blond hair, parted on the left. In the photograph he was laughing. He had a nice smile, she thought. She twisted the laptop round so that Theodore could see.

'What do you think of him?'

Theodore didn't bother to respond.

He didn't understand why Emily wasted so much time on dating websites, looking for a boyfriend. Cats couple at night, fulfil their desires and can be home for a good night's rest – free of commitment the next day. This human ideal of monogamous cohabitation was plain old miaowing up the wrong tree in his opinion. He glanced at the photograph of the potential suitor before meeting Emily's questioning gaze.

'Well?' she prompted, stroking him between the ears.

Theodore peered down at the chicken bones in the discarded tinfoil tray that had been left on the floor, wondering whether they were worth further investigation.

Emily clicked on the other photograph. In this one he was holding a cat. A black cat with white paws. A cat person, she thought and smiled.

He had signed off his message Jonathan.

She responded, asking him for clarification on what he did: 'What does a geologist actually do (apart from look at rocks!)…?'

She put the laptop on the coffee table and patted Theodore, who had decided that the remains of the chicken wings, stripped of their flesh, didn't warrant the effort. He decided to take possession of Emily's now vacant lap. But it didn't last long. He was soon deposited back on the seat of the sofa when Emily went to the kitchen to dish out her egg foo yung.

When she returned she already had a reply from Jonathan.

'I mainly dig holes with a JCB and supervise drilling. It's not as bad as it sounds! I live up near the racecourse. Do you live in South Bank?'

As Emily tapped out a response, glass shattered outside.

Emily didn't hear it for the whir of the old laptop, but Theodore's ears pricked up.

He got to his paws, jumped down from the sofa and went to investigate.

The Turkish couple at No.27 were fighting. Ahmet was a taxi driver. He worked for the local 'Crow Line' taxi firm. His wife Zeynep was pregnant with the couple's first child.

'You didn't come in till after two in the morning,' Zeynep said, her arms folded over her bump.

'What are you accusing me of?'

'I want to know where you were.'

'I had nothing to do with it. They arrested someone. It was in the newspapers, dear.'

'I just want to know where you were,' Zeynep repeated.

'You know it's the busiest time,' Ahmet said, 'after the pubs close. I cannot turn work away. Please do not get so excited. It's not good for the baby.'

'Not good for the baby!' Zeynep said, pointing her forefinger at her husband.

Ahmet looked at the broken glass scattered across the kitchen floor. He considered getting out the dustpan and brush, but knew his wife was not finished.

A fortnight earlier one of Zeynep's cats had gone missing. Zeynep had been beside herself. She had acquired the two Birman cats as kittens when she first came to England: a present from her then fiancé Ahmet. One she named Bal, *Honey* in Turkish, for her thick coat was the colour of set honey. The other she named Belle, after the heroine in *Beauty and the Beast*: Zeynep's favourite film.

She had spent many hours in the last two weeks walking the streets and back alleys of Clementhorpe and South Bank, calling out her missing cat's name. When Ahmet was not working he joined in the search. But, so far, they had been unable to find Bal.

The day before Peter Morris had been killed, Ahmet had voiced his suspicions: 'It might have been the old man with the pigeons down the street.'

'You think he's done something to Bal?'

'Cats kill birds,' he went on. 'People who keep birds don't like cats. Maybe it was him.'

Zeynep started crying, thinking the worst.

'I will go and ask him,' she said.

'No,' Ahmet said. 'I will speak to him.'

'And what will you say? Have you killed my cat?'

'No. of course not. I will just ask if he can check his shed. I will know from his reaction if he has done something to Bal.'

And that was how they had left it.

Ahmet now took his unfinished meal, placed it on the side by the sink.

'I was awake and you didn't come in till after two in the morning,' Zeynep went on.

'I told you. I had a fare to Malton at half past one. I was about to finish my shift. And I took the Malton fare – a very drunk couple. He fell asleep. I managed to get them out and then I came home… I am not going to turn work away when we need all the money we can get.'

'And you decided to do the laundry when you got in?'

'I was trying to be helpful. I put the washing machine on before I came upstairs. That's all. Is there a crime in that?'

'Only if you wanted to wash away the evidence.'

'You are crazy...' He raised his hands to his head. 'I didn't do anything to the old man. Now I must go to work. I don't want to hear any more of this.'

He grabbed his car keys from the side and walked out of the house, slamming the door behind him.

On the back wall Theodore sat with the remaining Birman cat, Belle. She had deep blue eyes and a tabby face. Her coat was the colour of smoked cheese; her legs and tail were pointed chocolate brown, her paws gloved in white.

Theodore had listened to the Turkish couple's argument with interest. It didn't take him long to tune into the Turkish language. To a cat each language is but one and the same. A Turkish Van cat can understand its English owner without a bilingual dictionary the same way a Persian cat living in Helsinki has no need of a Finnish grammar.

Theodore and Belle watched as Zeynep swept up the fragments of broken glass, struggling to reach the floor with the dustpan because of her swollen belly. She sat down at the kitchen table, her head resting on her folded arms. From the slight rising and falling of her shoulders Theodore realized that she was crying.

Belle jumped down from the wall and a moment later, she brushed against Zeynep's legs. Zeynep dropped a hand down and began stroking Belle's head. With her other hand, she wiped the tears from her cheeks.

Had Ahmet paid Peter Morris a visit on the night of the murder? Theodore wondered.

He closed his eyes in concentration. In addition to a dead man, a missing pigeon, there was now a missing cat.

How did that all fit together?

First Date

Within three days of first messaging Jonathan, Emily had agreed to meet him. Jonathan had suggested the Golden Ball in Bishophill at half past seven, leaving Emily with less than forty minutes to get ready when she got in from work.

She hurriedly squeezed a pouch of food into Theodore's bowl and replaced his water, while he brushed up against her legs, miaowing the whole time.

Then she poured herself a glass of wine and went upstairs to run a bath. Shortly after half seven, a second glass of wine inside her, she dashed out of the house and set off to the pub, a fifteen minute walk away.

If Emily went to the shop on the corner, she was usually gone for no more than ten minutes. When she had not returned after twenty, Theodore exited through the cat flap. A minute later he took up position behind the trellis that surrounded the Morris's yard.

Wendy Morris was sitting in the kitchen with her daughter, Laura. They were both dressed in black. The television was turned off. Peter Morris had been buried that afternoon at York Cemetery. A navy blue pram was parked in the yard, facing the back wall, but Theodore could not see inside. An old tea towel was hanging from the hood. The faded face of Richard III stared back gravely at Theodore. The pram stirred from time to time.

A middle aged man jogged past, a plastic nicotine inhaler in his hand. He smiled across at Theodore.

Theodore watched as he shuffled to the bottom of the alley and disappeared from sight. Then he turned his attention back to the kitchen window.

'Would you like a cup of tea?' Wendy asked her daughter.

Laura shook her head and then glanced at her watch.

'You can't go just yet,' Wendy said. 'How about a hot chocolate? You used to like a mug of hot chocolate.'

'No, thanks.'

'Your dad never liked hot chocolate either,' Wendy said. 'You've got that from him. Me, I like a mug of cocoa in the morning.'

'Do you have any coffee?' Laura said, a note of exasperation in her voice.

'I think I've got some Mellow Birds in the cupboard.'

'That'll be fine,' said Laura.

After she'd made her daughter a mug of milky coffee, she took a sheet of newspaper and placed it on the table.

Laura noticed that the newspaper was smeared with what appeared to be grease and smelled sharply of vinegar.

'Look at this,' Wendy said, pointing at the smudged headline. 'Three out of four new jobs go to foreigners, it says. No wonder you couldn't get owt when you finished.'

'You're beginning to sound like him now,' Laura said.

'But surely you want to get a job,' Wendy said. 'After you studied so hard at college.'

'We get by.'

'Well, if you did want to get a job, I could take Joseph while you're at work.'

'No,' Laura said. 'We're fine as we are.'

'You don't want to be stuck at home the rest of your life...'

'You've never shown any interest in Joseph before. You never even came to his christening.'

Wendy sighed. 'Things have changed now, haven't they? We can move on.'

Laura did not respond.

'Now that your dad is no longer around,' Wendy went on.

'I don't see what difference it makes. You could've come to your grandson's christening.'

'He wouldn't have it. You know that.'

'You could have stood up to him. Just because he was like that doesn't mean that you had to go along with it.'

Laura had raised her voice. She glanced through the kitchen window, to where the pram stood.

Mother and daughter sat in silence for a couple of minutes. Laura stared down at the sheet of newspaper on the table.

Theodore noticed Irene coming up the back alley. She opened the back gate and entered Wendy's yard.

'Yoo hoo!' she called, opening the back door.

Laura stood up.

'Are you leaving? Don't go on account of me.'

'Yes. I was just about to go,' Laura said.

'You look the spitting image of your mother,' Irene said. 'When she was your age... What with your red hair and all. You won't remember me. It's been a few years.'

'Of course I remember you, Irene,' Laura said, pushing her hair from her face. 'Do you still have your dog?'

'Rambo died. But I have a new dog now... Rocky. He's two years old now. Aye, I don't know where the time goes…'

'Rocky?'

'Like in the films... I do like a Stallone. Rocky. Rambo. Whatever. I'll watch it.'

Laura laughed. Then she said, 'I was about to leave.'

She walked past Irene, out into the yard. She turned the pram round and pushed it back into the house, the tea towel still hiding the contents.

As she circumnavigated the kitchen, Irene got in front of her. 'Let me have a look,' she said, plucking away the tea towel.

'He's sleeping,' Laura protested.

'I'm not going to wake him,' Irene said.

She bent over the pram.

'Ah… He's a beautiful lad,' she cooed.

Wendy approached but Laura had already begun to push the pram through into the front room, its curtains still closed.

'I really need to get going,' she said.

'Cheerio then,' called Irene.

'Remember what I said about the babysitting,' Wendy called after her.

'I remember,' Laura said, closing the door behind her.

Wendy picked up Laura's mug of undrunk coffee and poured it down the sink.

Sitting herself down at the kitchen table, Irene said, 'I haven't seen her for so long…'

Wendy went over to the kitchen cupboard.

'Would you like a drink of something?'

'What have you got?'

Wendy peered into the cupboard.

'Malibu?'

'Go on then,' Irene said. 'I haven't had a Malibu for ages.'

'It's Peter's. He used to like a glass of Malibu. He's hardly going to finish it now.'

Wendy poured Irene a generous tumbler full. She poured herself a finger of whisky.

'They still think that Craig did it for the money?' Irene said.

Wendy took a sip of whisky. 'What other reason could there be?'

'The papers say he was an oddball.'

'You just don't know who's living next to you these days.'

'It's not like the old days,' Irene said. 'Everybody used to know everybody's business back then.'

'They did that.'

Both women had a drink.

'He's back again,' Wendy said, nodding to her kitchen window.

'Who's that?'

'That girl's cat. He's eyeing up those pigeons. What's left of them.'

'He can't get in, can he?'

'No. Only through the gate… And he'll have to be quick to get past me.'

Irene looked to the window but couldn't make out the cat crouching behind the trellis; she had cataracts.

Emily brought Jonathan back to hers shortly after eleven o'clock. They had with them a plastic carrier bag containing half a crispy duck from the Lucky Twin Chinese takeaway.

She went to the kitchen and returned to the lounge with two plates, two glasses, knives, forks and spoons.

Theodore eyed the bag and sniffed its contents. A droplet of drool formed on his bottom lip.

'Is this your cat?' Jonathan said, patting Theodore heavily on the head.

'Yes. That's Theo,' Emily said, sitting down beside him.

Theodore stared up at Jonathan. He was sitting in his place... Where was he supposed to sit now? He paced the laminate floor, his tail raised, his ears folded flat.

Jonathan began to roll up a crispy duck pancake. Emily copied him, smearing plum sauce over a circular pancake, then added the dark brown crispy meat, spring onion and cucumber spears. Jonathan managed to roll his into a neat little cigar-shaped parcel. But when Emily tried, the pancake sprung apart, its filling spilling onto her lap.

She'd had three (or was it four?) glasses of wine at the Golden Ball. First date nerves, she'd reasoned.

'Here. I'll roll you one,' Jonathan offered. He quickly rolled her a pancake.

Emily ate the crispy duck roll in two mouthfuls, smearing her chin with plum sauce. 'That really is quite good,' she told him through a mouthful of food.

Theodore approached the plastic bag of food again. Just as he was about to stick his head inside to investigate, Jonathan pushed him away with the back of his hand.

'Hey,' he said. 'It's not for you.'

'You can have some later,' Emily said, picking the bag of food up and putting it up on the coffee table.

Theodore stared at the intruder. *Why should I have to wait? I was here first...*'

'I bet they still use monosodium glutamate,' Jonathan said. 'You know – MSG.'

'I thought that was banned.'

'It's not banned, I don't think. It's not good for you but it's not banned. In Japan they call it *umami*...'

'Umammammiii!' Emily said, and giggled. 'Can you roll me another?'

Theodore suddenly jumped up onto the coffee table. He spotted the dark brown meat in the tinfoil tray and made for it. But this time it was Emily who jumped up and grabbed him before he could snatch a sliver of crispy duck.

'No, you don't,' she told him. 'You've got your own food.'

Theodore let his body go limp, as she lifted him from the table.

Feel free to help yourself, he thought, retreating to a corner. *What's mine is yours and all that…*

'I didn't know what to expect,' Emily said, between bites of crispy duck roll.

'What's that?'

'A geologist… Maybe I was expecting someone in brown cords and a cardigan.'

Jonathan glanced down at his black jeans, relieved he had left his corduroy trousers in the drawer that evening.

After the duck pancakes had been eaten and a couple more glasses of wine had been drunk, Emily started crying.

'What is it?' Jonathan asked.

'Sorry,' Emily said. 'It's the wine…'

'Does wine make you cry?'

'That old man being murdered,' Emily said. 'I can't stop thinking about it.'

'Was that round here? I didn't realize.'

'Just behind,' Emily said, wiping her eyes. 'He lived on the corner opposite. I was the one who discovered the body. He was hit over the head with a cobblestone. And now my neighbour's been arrested. They think *he* did it…'

She nodded to the wall that separated her house from his.

'I didn't know.' Jonathan put his hand on her arm. 'You didn't say anything.'

'It's not really something you tell people when you first meet them… Oh, by the way, I discovered a dead body the other day. His head had been bashed in with a cobblestone…'

'Those blue cobblestones *are* heavy,' Jonathan said knowingly. 'They made them from slag from the old steelworks in Tyneside.'

'I didn't know that,' Emily said, rubbing her eyes.

After Emily and Jonathan went upstairs, Theodore jumped up onto the coffee table and finished off the last scraps of duck, then licked the droplets of grease from the silver carton. He wanted more, but there was no more to be had.

When Theodore climbed the stairs up to bed, he felt a faint buzzing in his head and a gnawing in his stomach. Must be that MSG, he thought.

Jonathan was on his side of the bed, his head bent back into the pillow, snoring loudly. Emily snorted in her sleep and murmured, 'Another one? I don't mind if I do.'

Theodore tried to get into the space between the two bodies, but he could not get comfortable. He climbed over Emily but there was not enough room for him on the edge of the bed. He clambered over Jonathan but the intruder chose that moment to turn on his side – sending Theodore onto the floor.

He paced the bedroom. Who was this person who had gate-crashed their lives?

For all he knew Jonathan could be the Clementhorpe Killer.

The intruder's jeans and socks were lying in a heap by the doorway to the en-suite bathroom. His boots were discarded by the foot of the bed. They were dark brown rancher style boots that a label claimed had been made in Tasmania.

Theodore sniffed at the intruding objects, his tail wagging with irritation.

Tuna Supper

Jonathan Fielder was from a small town called Market Weighton, located between York and Hull.

The town is famous for giving birth to a giant, Bill Bradley, and infamous for a witch, Peg Fyfe. Both fared badly. Bill died aged 33, having toured the country with a freak show that included a giant pig from nearby Sancton, a dwarf from Shiptonthorpe and a hunchback from Goodmanham. Peg was hanged after she skinned a young man alive. She survived the hanging by swallowing a wooden spoon, but was then slain by soldiers as she made her escape to York. Nowadays Peg has a real ale named after her; Bill a ring road.

Jonathan left the fairy tale-sounding town of Market Weighton when he was eighteen years old: he found it a bit small. He went to university in Leeds but found it a bit big. After he graduated he moved to York, which he found about right.

He woke at a quarter to seven and realized he was not in his own bed. Emily's alarm bleated from the corner of the room. She turned over, pulling the duvet with her, and silenced the alarm. She lay there and didn't say anything.

Jonathan rubbed his eyes and looked at his wristwatch, a much scratched stainless steel Casio.

'I'd better get off,' he said. 'I'm on a site on the other side of Bradford. It's a nightmare to get to.'

Emily didn't say anything.

Jonathan got out of bed and pulled on his jeans. He felt at his stubble, picked off some cat fluff and dropped it onto the floor.

The alarm went off again and Emily snoozed it again.

Jonathan went into the bathroom and splashed cold water onto his face. He looked at himself in the mirror. Clumps of cat fur were stuck in his hair. He picked them out and dropped them into the washbasin. His t-shirt, an obscure American indie band, was covered in a mesh of silver, grey and white fur. He picked off some of the bigger clumps and threw them onto the overflowing bin. He swore out loud. Then he said, 'I am absolutely covered in cat fur.'

'Maybe you shouldn't have slept in your t-shirt,' Emily said from below the duvet.

'Well, I did,' said Jonathan, thinking that maybe Emily wasn't a morning person. 'I didn't have the foresight to bring a pair of pyjamas,' he added.

'I thought you had a cat yourself,' Emily said.

'I used to. But he was black. I told you this last night, don't you remember.'

Jonathan's cat had been run over almost a year ago, but still the thought of his former companion brought a tear to his eye. He splashed more water onto his face, wanting to get outside as quickly as possible.

Emily glanced at her alarm clock. She really should have got up by now but was waiting for Jonathan to leave. The top of her mouth was dry and tacky, and she had a strange taste in her mouth. It must be that plum sauce, she thought, before wondering if she had any mouthwash in the house.

She watched as Jonathan crossed the room and, sitting on the corner of the bed, pulled on his boots. He swore again.

'My boots are wet,' he said. He took them off and put them to his face. 'I think your cat has weed in my boots.'

'Sorry,' Emily murmured from beneath the duvet. She looked again at her clock and hoped he would hurry up and leave.

Jonathan pulled his boots back on, swearing emphatically as he did so.

'Think I'm going to walk back through Scarcroft allotments,' he said. 'Wouldn't want anybody seeing me in this state.'

'Suit yourself,' Emily said. 'Bye.'

'Bye,' Jonathan almost barked.

A few seconds later Emily heard the front door open and slam shut. She jumped out of bed and began to run a bath.

Only then did Theodore crawl out from under the bed and make his presence known. In the ensuing rush to leave the house, he didn't want Emily to forget to feed him. Otherwise it would be a long hungry day.

While sitting in early morning traffic on the ring road that morning, Emily wondered if she would see Jonathan again.

She didn't have to wonder long. That evening she received a text message.

As soon as her mobile beeped, she picked it up from the coffee table and read: 'Had a great time last night... Would you like to meet up again this Friday?'

It was only Tuesday. She questioned how keen he actually was.

She waited twenty minutes, until the television show she was watching had finished, and then responded: 'Yes. Free Friday. Really enjoyed those crispy duck pancakes!'

She then noticed that her telephone was blinking. She reached over and played the message.

It was her mother.

'They've let him go,' she said. 'There's still a killer on the loose. Make sure you lock all your doors and windows tonight. Your dad says you should put something behind your back gate in case they try to force their way in...

'Oh, your father wants to say hello.'

'Hello,' her father said, and the message ended with a beep.

She picked up her laptop. She entered the address of the local newspaper. The headline confirmed that Craig Foster had been released.

'Clementhorpe Killer Still on the Loose', the newspaper headline announced.

The police had found no evidence to link Craig to the death of Peter Morris. Following a check on his bank accounts, it was discovered that Craig spent less than half of what he earned.

The other half remained in his bank account, accumulating interest. Craig Foster was not in any great need of money. The police could find no motive for him to have killed Peter Morris.

Emily shuddered to think that whoever had killed Peter Morris was still at large. And her neighbour, possibly the murderer, was probably back at home. Just the wall separating him from her, and not even a cavity wall at that.

'The police have stated that they are pursuing other lines of inquiry and if anybody has information they should contact them,' Emily read.

They have no idea who did it, she realised.

Emily thought back to the night Peter Morris was killed. She remembered being woken by Theodore in the early morning. The feathers dropped on her pillow. She wondered if she had overheard anything in the night. Had she heard arguing in the early hours? She couldn't remember anything but then her radio had been on.

She felt uneasy. She called for Theodore but he did not come.

She paced the front room. She went and checked that her back door was locked. She picked up the heavy pan from the side and practised swinging it at an imaginary intruder.

Back in the lounge, she picked up a magazine from the coffee table. She took in the headlines. 'My ninja kitten left me for dead'. 'My psychic dog has healing powers. Can he help you?' 'Car jacked! Then force fed meat pies.'

She threw the magazine across the room. 'Give me a break!' she cried.

She picked up the Chinese takeaway menu and grabbed her mobile. The Lucky Twin was engaged. She dialled again. On the fourth attempt she got through.

'I need a home delivery,' she blurted. 'Half a crispy duck... It's 17, Avondale Terrace.'

Theodore had heard Emily calling but chose to ignore her. He sat on the boundary wall with Craig's house. The parcel of grass was exposed, the white tent having been removed that morning.

The killer may well have thrown the cobblestone over the wall as he'd made his escape up the back alley. The entry to the alley at the top of the street was three hundred yards further up the hill and provided access from Avondale Terrace. The entry from Alcuin Terrace was located almost at the bottom of the hill, adjacent to the Morris's house.

If Peter Morris's killer didn't live on Avondale Terrace or Alcuin Terrace, he would have entered the back alley via the access closest to the Morris house, assuming the murder had been premeditated. Therefore whoever had killed Peter Morris had to live further up the back alley and not down it, Theodore concluded.

He jumped down into Craig's garden and, arching his back, signed his signature across the spot where he'd discovered the murder weapon. Mid-wee the backdoor opened and Craig appeared.

Theodore tightened his bladder and the stream of wee came to an abrupt stop. He felt the fur on his back bristling.

Craig froze. They faced each other.

'Wait there,' Craig said.

He turned and went back into his house. Theodore remained standing in the garden, his bushy tail held aloft.

He heard Emily calling again from inside his house. He stayed where he was.

It wasn't long before Craig returned. He placed a saucer of tuna on the edge of the lawn. Then he stood back into the kitchen doorway.

Theodore had never been given tuna to eat. Emily didn't even buy tuna-flavoured cat food. He sniffed the air and licked his lips.

Theodore approached. He wolfed down the saucer of tuna. He purred with thanks as Craig walked over. He rubbed himself against Craig's trousers, wondering if there was any tuna left. He let Craig pick him up and hold him to his chest.

Craig was soon overcome by emotion and began to cry. He sobbed into the cat's fur.

'Oh, mummy,' he cried. The tears streamed down his face. 'Why are they doing this to me?'

Theodore remained limp for a whole minute before writhing himself loose and jumping up onto the top of the boundary wall.

He watched as Craig returned inside his house and locked the door behind him.

Before Theodore returned home, he checked up on Wendy Morris. She was baking again.

Theodore sniffed the air. He picked out the savoury smells.

Meat pies, he deduced. *I wonder what meat?*

Then Irene came down the alley, pulled along by her dog Rocky straining at his lead.

A solitary magpie was perched on a television aerial near the bottom of the hill.

Irene spotted the black and white bird and raised a hand in salute. 'Good evening Mr Magpie,' she called. 'And how is your lady wife today?'

Irene knew that magpies paired for life. The solitary magpie was a widower; she didn't want to remind him of his loss. Yes, better to pretend, she said to herself.

Then she was dragged further down the alley by her dog.

Theodore looked across at the pigeon loft. He counted four pigeons. He glanced up at the sky and then the eaves of the house and the neighbouring houses.

Another pigeon had gone.

Bal and Belle

Friday evening Emily and Jonathan had their second date. They returned in the early hours, Jonathan carrying a small knapsack over his shoulder. While Emily was in the bathroom, Jonathan changed his t-shirt and put on a pair of pyjama bottoms. He then took from his bag a small hammer and placed it under his pillow. Theodore watched from the doorway, his eyes wide.

When Emily came out of the bathroom, Jonathan went in to brush his teeth.

Theodore sat down on the pillow which covered the hammer. When Emily got into bed he miaowed at her.

He's the killer, he wanted to tell her. He's going to bash your brains out while you sleep, like he did to Peter Morris…

'You can't stay there,' Emily said, stroking his head.

Jonathan came out of the bathroom. 'I can move him,' he said.

Theodore miaowed in protest.

'I'd better do it,' Emily said.

She crouched up on the bed and lifted her cat, but Theodore held on to the pillow with his claws and miaowed loudly. The pillow lifted from the bed with Theodore still attached, revealing the hammer underneath.

Now we're in trouble, thought Theodore, as he was deposited on the floor.

'What's that?' Emily asked, alarm in her voice.

'It's my hammer,' said Jonathan, picking up the hammer. 'You know – for breaking up specimens.'

'Specimens?'

'Yes, you know, bits of rock…'

'Well, what's it doing there?'

'To defend us… If someone broke in. I brought it just in case.'

'Well, you're not going to stand much chance with that little thing,' Emily said. She reached over and took out a hockey stick from below her side of the bed. 'Now you're going to get it!' she said with a grin.

Jonathan grabbed a pillow to use as a shield, as Emily advanced on her knees with hockey stick held high.

Theodore watched from the doorway as the play fight turned to a love match. There's always the spare bed, he thought, as he crossed the landing to the unlit front bedroom.

In the following weeks Theodore noted a change in the household dynamics. It began with Emily spending a lot more time in the bathroom a couple of evenings a week before disappearing outside, leaving Theodore to his own devices.

Half the time she would return with Jonathan and they would have a Chinese takeaway and a bottle of wine before going upstairs. Their antics in the bedroom were not conducive to a good night's rest. One Sunday he wasn't fed until nearly midday. It was completely unacceptable.

Other nights Emily would go out and not return. On these nights Theodore busied himself with his investigations. He had the double bed to himself but he missed Emily and slept with one ear listening out for her return.

Theodore did not like Jonathan; did not like it when he stayed over, and did not like it when Emily did not return home.

It was a Wednesday night and Emily was speaking to Jonathan on the phone. He was away the whole week, digging holes with a tracked excavator at a derelict steelworks in Cumbria. Theodore sat purring on her lap. He could stay in Cumbria for all he cared.

Emily was telling Jonathan how she had been applying for jobs in the centre of York. 'I can't stand that bloody ring road any longer,' she told him.

Outside a girl called out.

'I'll call you back later,' she told Jonathan.

She went upstairs and looked out of the back bedroom window. She saw a dark-haired girl, heavily pregnant, walking along the back alley.

Zeynep was calling for her missing cat Bal. She still hadn't given up hope that she would return, or that she would find her trapped in someone's shed or garage. Weeks had passed and the urgency of finding him had not lessened but increased as her pregnancy had advanced.

'Bal!' she called out. 'Come here, Bal.'

Emily opened her back gate and approached the other woman. 'Hi,' she said. 'I was wondering what you were shouting.'

'Bal,' Zeynep said. 'It means 'honey' in Turkish. She's one of my cats. I have two. They are sisters. But Bal has gone missing. I am trying to find her.'

'My cat goes missing for a few hours but he always comes back,' Emily said. 'I'm sure yours will too.'

'Bal's been gone for weeks now. I've put posters up. I've looked all over for her... I can't find her anywhere. But I know she is alive. Somewhere.'

'Can I help you look for her?' Emily offered.

'Yes, of course... Please.'

As they walked up the cobbled alley, Emily said, 'Your English is so good. I wish I knew a foreign language.'

'I studied English at university in Ankara,' she said. 'When I came here I hoped to do my Masters at York University. I wanted to be a teacher. But we don't have money for study, and they probably wouldn't let me in anyway.'

'I'm sure you still could if you really wanted.'

'I don't think so,' said Zeynep, pointing at her stomach, her eyes cast upwards. 'Not now anyway.'

Emily found out that Zeynep's husband Ahmet worked as a taxi driver, working split shifts: mornings and evenings. For over an hour they walked the streets, calling out the missing cat's name and chatting together.

They cut through the allotments, skirted the racecourse and passed by the Knavesmire pub. Then back down Queen

Victoria Street, passing the fish and chip shop in the heart of South Bank. Emily glanced inside and spotted an old man in a white apron standing behind the counter – his shop empty of customers.

Emily noticed that Zeynep had slowed down. 'Shall we turn back?' she suggested.

'Yes, OK.'

They turned down a side street, and began walking back towards Clementhorpe.

Emily smelled the Lucky Twin before she saw it.

The Chinese takeaway was located in the middle of the residential district, where not a tree was visible. Red brick terraced housing fronted directly onto the pavement. Tarmac roads were lined with cars parked on both sides.

In front of the takeaway a sign bore the name 'The Lucky Twin' in white letters on an emerald green background. In the window an A3 sheet of brown paper had been sellotaped. 'Now Fish and Chip "Special" – for Retail'.

There were about twenty people inside the little shop waiting for their food.

That'll be why the fish and chip shop isn't doing so well, thought Emily. She looked across the street at the takeaway. Her stomach rumbled. 'I haven't eaten,' she said. 'Will you be all right walking back? Or you can wait for me.'

'I'll be fine,' Zeynep said. 'It's not far.'

'As long as you're sure.'

'Yes, of course.'

Zeynep continued along the street, and Emily crossed the road to the Lucky Twin.

The Chinese woman was taking an order over the telephone, so Emily busied herself looking at the menu on the white board although she knew what she was going to have. What she couldn't decide was whether to have a quarter or a half. Then she noticed the price. A half, 'special' crispy duck was £14.50. She was certain that when she and Jonathan had come in a couple of weeks ago it had been £12.50.

She decided to settle for a quarter.

Sue Wong said into the receiver, 'There is forty minute delay for home deliveries. We are very busy today...' She then scribbled the order onto a chit of paper, slapped it onto the service hatch, and, turning to Emily, said 'Yes, please?'

'Crispy duck?' Emily asked.

'A quarter or a half?'

'Just a quarter,' Emily said, retrieving her purse from her handbag.

Almost an hour later she got her crispy duck home.

As she entered her house, she stepped over a brown manila envelope. She didn't pick it up. She hurried on into the kitchen. She opened up the silver carton and began pushing the crispy brown meat into her mouth, ignoring the polystyrene container of plum sauce and plastic wrapped pancakes.

Theodore appeared at her feet and began to rub up against her calves. He stared up at her with wide hungry eyes.

'You wait your turn,' she told him, wagging a greasy forefinger before pushing more meat into her mouth.

She carried her dinner into the front room and flicked on the television. She had eaten a third of the meat before she opened the other containers.

She ripped open the polythene that held the pancakes, smeared over the plum sauce with her finger, then laid out the cucumber and spring onion. She added a clump of meat, folded up the bottom, then rolled the pancake into a cigar. After her third roll she looked down at Theodore.

He sat at her feet, drooling onto the laminate flooring.

She looked in the silver tray. There were a few shreds of duck left. She handed over the remains. 'Sorry,' she said guiltily. 'I must have been hungry.'

There was an uneasiness that seemed to stem from her stomach. She glanced at her watch and wondered whether to return to the takeaway for another quarter. The uneasiness began to increase. She paced the ground floor of her house, beads of sweat beginning to prick out on her head.

She picked up the brown envelope from the door mat and removed its contents. There were two sheets of A4 paper. A pink post-it note was stuck on the top one.

'Thought these might be useful,' her mother had written on the heart-shaped post-it note.

One photocopied sheet contained a breakdown of the Cabbage Soup Diet, the other the Dukan Diet.

Evidently her mother had noticed that she'd put on a bit of weight in the last few weeks, since Peter Morris's death. She went and put the papers into the recycling bin.

Back in the front room, she noticed the red LED on her telephone flashing, telling her someone had left her a message. She knew it would be her mother.

She played the message: 'Did you get the leaflets I left you,' her mother said. 'I thought they might be useful. I went to the library today…

'This new boyfriend of yours,' she went on, 'I hope you have done a full police background check on him. You never know these days. And did you say he was a geologist? I bet he has grubby fingers… Oh your father wants to say hello.'

'Hello', her father said. The answer phone beeped. Then there was just the silence of her front room.

The uneasiness in her stomach had become a general dissatisfaction with her life. She hated her job. She was now ill at ease in her own house, and did not even feel comfortable in her own skin. If only she had another quarter of crispy duck, but now it was too late.

She finished the bottle of wine, poured herself a glass of water and went upstairs.

She lay in bed and thought of her neighbour who had been arrested for killing the pigeon man and later released. He was probably sleeping on the other side of her bedroom wall contemplating who he was going to kill next.

She thought of the Turkish woman, Zeynep, and her missing cat, Bal. She thought of her own cat Theodore, who had been accused of taking that stupid pigeon by Wendy Morris. She thought of Peter Morris, who had had his head bashed in. She reached under the bed and reassured herself that her hockey stick was there.

She wished Jonathan was with her. She texted him: 'Hello, are you awake?' and when he didn't respond after ten minutes she understood that he was no doubt sleeping in his hotel room on the other side of the country. She turned over and began to cry into her pillow.

Downstairs Theodore lapped at the aromatic duck grease that coated the tin foil container left on the floor. Then he heard Emily crying to herself from the bedroom upstairs. He finished the last droplets of grease and padded upstairs.

'Oh, Theo,' Emily said, when he settled on the pillow beside her. 'What's happening to me?'

Theodore tried to reassure her. *I'll find out*, he purred. *I'll get to the bottom of it.*

The Art of the Mundane

Theodore was sitting on the boundary wall of Michael's house, within a tangle of overgrown ivy. The sash window at the back of the house was open a couple of inches, and Theodore could hear classical music. Michael was working on his drawing.

Theodore watched as Michael added tiny pencil marks to an incredibly detailed sketch of the back alley, looking down from the top of the hill to the church at the bottom. He was now working on the clematis that hung over Theodore and Emily's back wall. He used the little wooden mallet as a rest, so that he wouldn't smudge his work. So that's what the mallet's for, thought Theodore.

Michael took a break. In the kitchen he poured himself a glass of green liquid. He winced as he swallowed the wheatgrass and Theodore winced with him.

Neither man nor cat was meant to eat greens, thought Theodore. They were only good for clearing out your digestive tract. Even dogs knew that. He watched as Michael drained the contents of the small glass, his face screwed up.

Michael turned and faced the kitchen window, his face still contorted. He spotted Theodore perched in the ivy and hissed through his teeth at the cat. He returned to the lounge and began to apply delicate shading to the clematis.

Theodore closed his eyes. He wasn't overly fond of Michael either.

He opened his eyes again when he heard a door slam.

Michael swore. A thick black pencil line now extended from the clematis down to the hexagonal cobblestones outlined in the foreground. He took a deep breath, snapped his pencil into two and threw both pieces at the wall.

'What's up?' Philip said, entering the room.

'Look what you've made me do.'

'Oh dear,' said Philip, surveying the picture. 'It'll rub out, won't it?'

'Yes,' Michael said. 'I think I can fix it. But do you have to slam the door every time you come in?'

'Sorry Mikey,' Philip said. He walked into the kitchen and opened the fridge. 'Who's going to buy a drawing of a back alley, anyway?'

'Somebody who appreciates art,' Michael said. 'That's who.'

'So how many of these pictures have you actually sold?'

'It's not all about money,' Michael said. 'If it were, I'd be a stockbroker or something, you know, in the City...'

'I just can't see you becoming famous drawing pictures of back alleys.'

'It's about seeing the beauty in the mundane,' Michael said.

'Mundane being the appropriate word,' Philip said, pouring a glass of milk.

'One day I will be appreciated. You wait… They will know who I am.'

'I saw a nice pair of trainers in town,' Philip said, changing the subject. 'Two hundred pounds though.' He sucked in air through his teeth.

'You've got a new pair of trainers,' Michael said, looking down at Philip's feet.

Philip was wearing a pair of bright red trainers.

'Yes, but these were yellow,' Philip said. 'I don't have a pair of yellow ones.'

'Do you need a pair of yellow ones?'

'Well, I don't *need* a pair of yellow trainers,' Philip said. 'I just thought they looked good. They would go with that silk shirt you bought me the other week…'

Philip sat down at the table in the lounge. He took a drink of milk. He looked out of the back window.

'Every time I come round here,' he said, a thin milk moustache on his top lip, 'I think about what happened that morning. That poor old man being killed. They still haven't caught him, have they?'

'No,' Michael said, his pencil poised above the paper. 'It was a terrible thing to happen.'

'Yes, terrible,' Philip said. He looked again out of the window, his eyes narrowed to slits. 'A terrible thing to happen.'

From within the ivy Theodore yawned. He was wasting his time investigating this pair. He couldn't imagine either of them hurting a fly; let alone a little old man.

The Loneliness of the Undercover Cat

As any seasoned detective will tell you, surveillance work is tedious and tiring. The endless hours spent listening to conversations. Never knowing when something pertinent might slip from an unguarded mouth. Never knowing when a fragment of conversation may become relevant to the investigation later. The hours spent enduring the shifting weather. Not being able to slip home for a bite of food or sip of water for fear of missing a slip of the tongue.

It was essential but dull work.

Anyone passing would think that Theodore was just a cat sitting on a wall, and not a detective carrying out covert surveillance. He understood that this was what made him superior to the police. If a police officer was sitting on your back wall, staring at you through your kitchen window, you would probably have something to say.

Theodore jumped down into the back alley and up onto the top of the wall on the other side. Through the trellis he saw the pigeon loft, its white paintwork glistening in the spring sun.

He counted only three pigeons. They flitted in and out of their roosts, fluttered over the yard and rested on the eaves of the houses. There had been half a dozen. Now there were only three. They were restless.

What was happening to the pigeons? Theodore wondered.

Through the trellis he watched as Irene and Wendy ate dinner at the kitchen table. A radio on the kitchen windowsill was tuned to Minster FM. The women chewed on their food as the news headlines were read out.

New plans had been announced for the old Terry's chocolate factory, located to the south of Clementhorpe; alcohol-fuelled violence had erupted in York city centre following yesterday's horse racing, and finally a multiple pile up on the A64 was causing delays on the eastbound carriageway, back to Tadcaster.

There was no mention of Peter Morris's murder, noted Theodore. There had been no developments. Nothing new. It was no longer news.

Wendy stood up and approached the window. She turned off the radio and returned to her dinner.

'Who'd have thought it?' Irene said. 'They'll be building houses at Terry's.'

'Better than it being left derelict,' Wendy said.

'Aye,' Irene said. 'It's been closed a few years now.'

'I knew the factory would close as soon as they stopped making them chocolate oranges,' Wendy said. 'It was only a matter of time.'

'Aye,' Irene agreed. 'It was only a matter of time.'

Irene's husband had been forced into redundancy before he'd reached sixty, after the production of chocolate oranges had moved to Poland. Too old to find another job, he'd idled around the house for a few months before breathing his last during a particularly eventful *Crimewatch*.

Wendy was bent over a plate of leftover chicken, and chips Irene had bought from Mr White's fish and chip shop. Crumpled newspaper and greaseproof paper lay on the kitchen side.

'He's struggling,' Irene told Wendy Morris. 'I was the only one in.'

'He can't compete with those Chinese.' Wendy said. 'When they started doing fish and chips, it was the beginning of the end for Frank White.'

Irene sighed and forked a chip into her mouth.

'It's only a matter of time before he sells up,' Wendy went on, chewing on a mouthful of chicken and chips. 'It'll be a kebab shop by the end of the year, mark my words.'

'The Wongs cook everything from frozen,' Irene said. 'They import their fish from Russia. They serve their chips in polystyrene trays.'

'He can't afford to keep going,' Wendy said. She took a mouthful of tea to clear her mouth.

'The chips from the Chinese don't taste the same, I tell you,' Irene said. 'It's like I've always said…Two Wongs don't make a White…' She slapped the kitchen table, laughing.

'That joke wasn't funny the first time you told it,' Wendy said deadpan.

After they had finished their tea, Wendy took their mugs to the sink, and adding them to the greasy plates, filled the sink with hot water. She pulled on her pink rubber gloves. She took the chicken carcass from the fridge and, with the aid of a small, sharp knife, began to strip the remaining meat from the carcass. She added the chicken meat to a plastic margarine tub on the side. She then slid the carcass into her kitchen bin. She began to wash the dishes.

'So the police are no closer to finding out who did it?' Irene asked.

'There's no new leads,' Wendy said, her back to Irene. 'That's what they told me.'

'When they found the murder weapon I thought that would be it.'

'Maybe it *was* that Craig Foster. But there was no evidence to place him at the scene,' Wendy said. 'And no motive.'

'Sometimes people don't need a motive,' Irene said. 'They kill for the sake of it. There are some strange ones about these days.'

'Yes,' agreed Wendy.

'Whoever did it must have planned it,' Irene said. 'That's why they couldn't find any fingerprints. They would have worn gloves.'

Wendy Morris turned round. Suds fell from her pink rubber gloves onto the linoleum floor.

Theodore stared at the pink clad hands which continued to drip suds onto the floor. *Had Wendy clobbered her husband wearing those pink rubber gloves?*

'I think it's time for our soap,' Wendy said.

Theodore got to his paws and stretched. He walked along the wall. Ahead of him a stocky black cat blocked his path.

Theodore stopped in his tracks and held the other cat's stare for a moment.

They knew each other by sight. They knew each other by scent. They were enemies, and always would be. Arthur, the black cat, was not going to make way for Theodore.

Arthur looked across at the remaining pigeons. He looked at Theodore.

Arthur was an unneutered tom. Like all civilized cats Theodore was neutered. He looked on Arthur as some sort of primitive species, driven by baser instincts. As Theodore held the intellectual high ground, he understood enough to make way for this coarse feline.

Theodore jumped down onto the cobbles of the back alley and padded towards his own house. Without turning round, he jumped up onto his back wall and a second later was back within the safety of his own territory.

From the front of the house he heard Emily's Beetle pull to an abrupt halt and Leonard Cohen come to a stop mid-lyric ('But I swear by this song…').

A few seconds later he was at the front door, ready to greet her.

Fortune Monkey: No Good

'I still can't get through.'

Emily paced the living room, her mobile phone pressed to her ear, her sandals clacking on the laminate floor.

'Why can't we just call another takeaway?' Jonathan said. 'I've got some numbers on my phone.' He was sitting on the sofa, remote control in hand – flicking through the endless television programme listings.

Emily slumped down on the sofa beside him causing him to rise a couple of inches. She said, 'They can get really busy. That'll be why they're not answering… Maybe they have stopped doing home deliveries… I think we should walk over there. It won't take long.'

Jonathan had been up at half past five that morning, and had spent all day in the bright sunshine of a car park in the Midlands, logging tubes of soil returned to the earth's surface by a small percussive drilling rig. He didn't want to walk half a mile back across South Bank, only to stand and wait for a takeaway when they could easily telephone another takeaway and have it delivered in minutes. But Emily had already got to her feet.

He reluctantly got up from the sofa, pulled on his boots. He drained his glass of wine. 'All right,' he said. 'Let's go and get some crispy duck!' straining to sound upbeat.

He followed Emily out of the house and, taking her hand in his, they began to walk to the top of Avondale Terrace, his feet sweaty and sore within the confines of his boots.

As he walked he felt his palm grow damp. He could feel the heat emanating from Emily's palm. He removed his hand from hers, hoping she didn't notice.

Theodore followed, keeping at least two cars behind, so that they didn't realize they were being tailed. He would find out the source of the crispy duck, he thought. He might even get to swipe a whole portion for himself. He licked his lips.

The road was lined on both sides with parked cars, but compared to the back alleys, he felt exposed. He trotted between the cars, breaking into a gallop in any extended gaps.

When Emily and Jonathan got to the top of Avondale Terrace, he waited until they were at least thirty yards ahead before sprinting across Southlands Road. His technique for crossing roads was simple: run across as fast as you can: the less time spent crossing meant the less chance of getting run over.

The evening sky was overcast and the air heavy with a storm that would not break until the early hours of the morning. Emily felt the tension building in her head, as the atmospheric pressure rose. She hoped it would not develop into a migraine.

She was sweating and she regretted not putting on deodorant before Jonathan came round. Fortunately she was wearing a white linen blouse which she hoped did not show the damp below her arms. She'd started to sweat more than she used to. She'd gone back on the pill and that was probably the reason.

They walked down Nunthorpe Grove, a wide residential street lined with squat 1930's semis. The locals call the road the Big Dipper, as it goes up and down like a camel's back.

Where there were long gaps in the parked cars, Theodore took to the front gardens, darting and diving through gaps in hedges and fences, keeping a safe distance behind Emily and Jonathan. There was definitely an art to not being seen, he thought, as he dashed across a gravel driveway and under a transit van.

There were streetlights on either side of the road. On each mast there was an A4 sheet of paper, contained within a plastic envelope. The makeshift poster read:

MISSING CAT
HER NAME IS BAL
PLEASE CALL ZEYNEP ON 07515 623070
FOR ANY INFORMATION
"LITTLE REWARD"

There was a photograph of the blue-eyed Birman cat below the text.

'She still can't have found her cat,' Theodore heard Emily say.

'She won't if she is offering little reward,' Jonathan said.

'I think she means a small reward, stupid.'

Jonathan pointed out two houses near the top of Nunthorpe Grove. 'They had to be rebuilt,' he said. 'The original houses were destroyed by a German bomb that was dropped nearby.'

'I didn't know,' Emily said.

'The houses were badly damaged,' Jonathan went on. 'They were on fire, so the fire brigade came and put out the fire.'

'Was anybody hurt?'

'There were seven young female cadets billeted in the house,' Jonathan said, as they approached South Bank Avenue. 'But they could only account for six. When they drained the bomb crater of firewater, they discovered the body of the seventh. She'd drowned…'

From behind them, there was the screech of brakes.

They turned and saw a pastel blue Fiat that had come to a stop in the middle of the road. Then they saw Theodore flattened against the road. The smell of burnt rubber hung in the air.

'Theodore!' Emily cried. She ran over and picked him up.

Theodore stared back into Emily's face, his eyes bulging, his heart thumping. He began to wriggle himself free.

'I think he's all right,' Emily said, holding onto him tightly.

The door of the Fiat swung open and a woman with short dark hair got out.

'Is that cat yours?' the woman asked, her voice high-pitched, verging on hysterical.

'He must have followed us,' Emily said, still clutching her cat.

'I could have killed him,' the other woman said.

Emily hugged Theodore to her chest, beginning to cry. 'I'm sorry,' she said.

'He gave me the fright of my life.'

'I'm sorry,' Emily said again.

'I'm just glad I managed to stop… I have a cat of my own.'

'I think we'd better get him home,' Jonathan said.

The woman got back into her car and drove away in first gear, lighting a cigarette as she went.

Emily and Jonathan crossed back over South Bank Avenue.

Emily glanced behind. The Lucky Twin was only round the corner. She sighed, holding tightly onto Theodore.

Theodore sniffed the air. He could smell Chinese food. So close, but yet so far, he thought as he was carried home.

Back at Emily's house, Jonathan asked, 'What are we going to do for dinner now? I'm starving.'

'Well… what do you suggest?' Emily said.

'I have a number for another Chinese takeaway on my mobile,' Jonathan said. 'I can call right now.'

'Are you sure they'll do the special crispy duck?' Emily asked, Theodore purring on her lap.

'They all do,' Jonathan replied.

He already had his mobile out and was scrolling through his contacts. 'You won't notice the difference… Here we go. Fortune Monkey.'

'Fortune Monkey?'

'Yes. That's what it's called. Look: I've had food from them before and it's fine… And it's much cheaper than the Lucky Twin.'

Emily chewed on the duck rolls unenthusiastically. They tasted of nothing. Perhaps cardboard if she was feeling generous, but she wasn't.

While they ate, Theodore took care of his personal hygiene.

'I didn't know your cat could play the tuba,' Jonathan said, nodding over at Theodore.

'He can't,' Emily said. Then, noticing what Theodore was doing, said, 'Oh, I see.'

The air grew heavier. On the television Jonathan had put on a Swedish crime drama that he'd said was good. He was busy eating his way through a portion of prawn toast.

Emily had feigned interest in the television programme, but had given up on it two minutes after it had started. She didn't want to put her glasses on in front of Jonathan and was unable to read the subtitles without them. She finished her wine and went into the kitchen to refill her glass.

Theodore followed her into the kitchen. He was not keen on Nordic Noir either.

He'd already put the near miss behind him. He hadn't been hurt. He'd learned a lesson about crossing the road. It was not such a big deal, he thought to himself. He still had eight lives left after all.

He miaowed up at Emily, who was tidying up the remains of the Fortune Monkey meal. She dropped some strips of duck onto the floor in front of him. He sniffed at them but left them lying on the tiled floor. Emily was right: Fortune Monkey just wasn't the same as the Lucky Twin.

'I don't think Theodore's feeling well,' Emily said when she returned to the front room. 'I think he's traumatised. Maybe I'll take him to the vet's tomorrow morning.'

'He seems fine to me,' Jonathan said, not looking away from the television.

'He may have internal injuries,' Emily said.

Jonathan shrugged. 'So, what do you think of the Fortune Monkey crispy duck?' he said.

'I think I prefer the Lucky Twin.'

'It tastes all right to me,' Jonathan said.

'It lacks something…' she said. 'It's not the same as the Lucky Twin.'

'They probably don't use the MSG.'

'No,' Emily said. 'They probably don't.'

'We've still got the fortune cookies.'

Jonathan handed one of the foil wrapped shells to Emily, and then took the other for himself. He broke open the sweet and read: 'Your relationships will come to nought and you will die a painful death.'

Emily opened hers. 'You will lose what is most precious to you,' it said. 'You will never be able to replace it.'

They both crumpled up their slips of paper and tossed them onto the coffee table without saying anything to the other.

Theodore chewed on the tag of one of Jonathan's boots, which he'd left by the side of the sofa. He soon succeeded in eating through the cotton loop that Jonathan used to pull his boot on. He'd made a start on the other boot when Jonathan noticed what he was up to.

'Hey, get off!' Jonathan shouted and swiped a hand at Theodore.

'Don't you touch my cat,' Emily started.

There followed a brief argument which ended with Jonathan pulling on his boots with what remained of the tags and walking out, the front door slamming shut behind him.

From beneath the sofa, Theodore listened to his footsteps recede, as he stomped up the hill.

As soon as he'd gone, Emily glanced at her watch. The Lucky Twin would be closed by now. She finished the bottle of wine and went upstairs to bed.

In the middle of the night, the storm broke and heavy rain fell. Emily lay awake in bed, the sheets damp beneath her. She began to feel the tension in her head dissipate. She turned over and stroked Theodore, who purred reassuringly by her side.

In his own bed half a mile away, Jonathan woke several times in the night. The rain lashed his window. He struggled to sleep.

The next morning, as he drank his coffee before setting off to work, he sent Emily a text.

'Sorry re last night,' he wrote. 'You were right. Fortune Monkey: No good.'

A Rainy Day

It rained all the next day.

Theodore stayed inside, only going out to empty his bowels in the covered litter tray in the corner of the yard.

At least it's covered, he thought, listening to the rain patter on the plastic lid.

Then he went back inside and watched *Columbo*.

Miniature Ottoman Houses and Black Furry Underpants

Ahmet Akbulut had a hobby. In the afternoons between his morning and evening shifts, he built miniature Ottoman houses.

Almost all of the elegant old timber houses back in his hometown of Zonguldak, on the Black Sea coast, had been burned down or bulldozed, only to be replaced by nondescript concrete apartment blocks, two to four storeys high.

As a boy he had dreamed of becoming an architect and reviving traditional forms of domestic building. But then he'd had to go out to work at fourteen, after his father's ill health meant he could no longer work at the local coal mine. Ahmet had left school and abandoned his dream.

But not quite.

In the intricate models he built in the spare bedroom, soon to be a nursery, his dream survived. At the moment, he was building a doll's house. He secretly hoped his wife was carrying a girl.

In the afternoons, he glued matchsticks to matchsticks with balsa cement, cut rectangular holes for windows in corrugated cardboard walls, and, with his trusty craft knife, cut out fingernail-shaped roof tiles from thin sheets of balsa wood.

On six separate shelves in the back bedroom were six completed miniature Ottoman houses. Each house had taken him a year to construct. They represented six years of working in England: first delivering fast food for a pizza outlet and then as a taxi driver. Each month he sent money back to his family in Turkey.

When the baby arrived he would have to find somewhere else to build his houses, Zeynep had warned him; the table where he now worked would be for nappy changing. He would put a window into the sloping shed roof, he thought, gazing out across the yard and catching the stare of a large grey fluffy cat sitting on the back wall.

Theodore noticed Ahmet look up from his work and out of the window. Most times he looked in the same direction. To a house on the other side, a little further up the hill.

Zeynep carried a laundry basket out into the yard. Belle followed a moment later and lay down on the concrete, as Zeynep hung out the clothes to dry.

After a minute, she turned to the window of the back bedroom. 'Ahmet!' she shouted up.

'Yes, dear,' Ahmet shouted down.

'Have you been stealing my pegs?'

'Pegs? No, dear. What would I want with your pegs?'

He looked across the table to the shoebox where he stockpiled his materials. Inside he had acquired several wooden pegs that he was going to transform into a peg family. He had already drawn on faces and hair with a permanent marker. He had also swiped a couple of pairs of black lace knickers from Zeynep's underwear drawer. She hadn't noticed, as she hadn't been able to fit into them for some time. Ahmet planned to create a black silk dress for the peg grandmother and aunties. But he'd shied away from the task, thinking it may well be beyond his capabilities.

He turned his attention back to the balsa wood tiles and cut out another half dozen. He hoped to have one side of a roof tiled before he started his evening shift. His mobile beeped from within his jeans pocket. He read the message and, smiling to himself, looked outside.

Theodore followed his stare and noticed a pair of blue satin curtains twitch.

Ahmet responded to the text, replaced his mobile in his jeans, and then picked up his tube of balsa cement once more. But before he could glue another tile onto the roof, Zeynep shouted up at him once more, her voice edgier and higher pitched.

'Yes, dear?' he called down.

'Get down here now!'

As Ahmet came out of the back door, Theodore saw that Zeynep was holding up a pair of white underpants.

'What are these? she said, waving the pants at Ahmet.

'My underpants?' Ahmet said, palms outstretched.

'No, these?'

She plucked at the pants. In her fingers she held a pinch of short black hairs.

Ahmet looked at the hairs. 'They are little black hairs,' he said. 'So? I have black hair. They are my little hairs. Is it an offence to leave some little hairs in my underpants?'

'It's fur. Not hair,' Zeynep said. 'I do know the difference.'

'We have cats, don't we? It is just a bit of cat fur. Gets everywhere.'

'We have Belle,' Zeynep said. 'But she is not black. If you hadn't noticed.'

'What are you accusing me of?'

'I want to know how you got black fur on your underpants when we don't have a black cat.'

'Please, Zeynep,' Ahmet said. 'It is all in your head. Hormones because of the baby.'

Zeynep swore, then kicked over the laundry basket, sending its damp contents spilling onto the ground. Then she marched back inside the house, slamming the door behind her.

Ahmet picked up the basket and finished hanging out the washing – running out of pegs before he had finished.

Theodore watched him from the back wall. In the back bedroom window he spotted Belle looking down at Ahmet.

Then he sensed another presence. He turned round, and further up the hill, on the other side of the alley, he was met by Arthur's amber stare. Arthur was sitting on the back wall of the house with the blue satin curtains. It was his house.

The black cat did not blink instead its stare bore into Theodore.

Theodore looked away, down the hill.

How had Arthur's fur got on Ahmet's underpants? he wondered.

Carbolic Soap and Tuna Fish

From on top of the chest in the bay window, Theodore could see to the end of the street. He spied Wendy crossing the road, on her way to the shops; her shopping trolley bumping along behind. Theodore glanced at the DVD player on the shelf below the television. 14:24.

At 15.07 he spotted Irene being pulled across the road by Rocky. Ahmet pulled away in his taxi at 16.15 to begin his evening shift. At 17.07 Craig Foster glided to a halt on his bicycle in front of his house. He glanced up and down the street before unlocking his door and pushing his bicycle inside.

Tuna time, Theodore thought.

He got to his paws, stretched and a minute later exited the cat flap.

Craig Foster usually arrived home before Emily by about twenty minutes. Before he met Theodore he'd only gone into his back garden on a Tuesday to put out his rubbish when he remembered, which wasn't very often. But now after arriving home each day, he opened the backdoor and took out a saucer of tuna for his neighbour's cat.

Theodore rubbed against Craig's legs, letting himself be patted on the head before wolfing down the tuna.

Craig took his tuna sandwich to the back room, where he sat at the table and ate it in the semi dark. After his sandwich, he went to the bathroom where he remained for ten minutes.

Theodore continued his search of Craig's house while Craig was in the bathroom. He'd searched most of the house but had yet to find anything to incriminate Craig with Peter Morris's murder. Not even a pigeon feather.

However, Theodore knew Craig was lying about one thing. He knew that he was not as interested in stargazing, as he had made out to the police. If he hadn't been looking up at the stars, what had he been looking at?

He climbed the stairs in seconds and paused on the landing. The curtains in the bedrooms were permanently closed but the bathroom door was ajar and light leaked in through frosted glass. Yesterday Theodore had searched the bathroom: an unpleasant task he was glad to get over.

He now climbed the stairs to the attic room. Magazines and papers lay scattered across grey carpet tiles, many of which lay open to display photographs of the human anatomy, focussing primarily on the sexual organs. Theodore arched his eyebrows and continued his search.

Under the eaves at the front, several monitors and out-dated computers were stored along with boxes of cables for the now redundant machinery.

There was a desk against the chimney breast on which sat a computer monitor, its screen blank. The computer stood on the floor beside the desk and whirred quietly to itself. A black metal waste paper bin, overflowing with used tissues stood next to the computer. Empty tissue boxes and toilet rolls lay scattered across the floor.

Human behaviour sometimes bemused Theodore; sometimes it just saddened him. He decided against a detailed examination of the contents of the bin.

He jumped up onto the desk and stood in front of the monitor. He dabbed at the mouse which sat next to the keyboard. Suddenly the screen sprang to life. *'SPANKING TIME!'* the website shouted in fat pink letters.

Three young females crouched in a row, their rear ends raised.

As a kitten Theodore had raised his behind to allow his mother to inspect his nether regions, an honour he now bestowed on his human Emily from time to time. However, he doubted Craig's interest in behinds was hygiene related.

A chair in the middle of the room faced a Velux window, set into the sloping roof. In front of the chair a telescope was attached to a tripod.

Theodore remembered Craig's astrological slip to the police officer when they were taking him away for questioning. He noted that the telescope was not pointing up towards the sky but below the horizon. He jumped across onto the chair seat and then up onto the back of the chair. Balancing on the thin chair back, he lined up his sight with the telescope. He made out the back bedroom window of a house on the other side of the alley, a few houses further up. The window had blue satin curtains.

Theodore noted that the curtains were halfway between open and closed, and the window was open a couple of inches at the bottom. From within the darkened room a pair of amber eyes stared back at him.

Downstairs the toilet flushed. Theodore jumped down from the chair and raced downstairs.

When Craig emerged from the toilet Theodore was by the door, licking the empty saucer. Craig picked him up and hugged him to his chest. 'See you tomorrow, little man,' he said.

He put Theodore back down and picked up the saucer.

He gave Theodore a little wave before going back into his house, closing and locking the backdoor behind him. He would not leave his house again until the next morning.

Theodore jumped up onto the boundary wall. He looked across at the houses opposite.

He understood that Craig was not interested in astronomy, but was undertaking his own surveillance. But why?

From the front of the house, Theodore heard Emily park her car. Michael Jackson came to an abrupt end ('Just to tell you once again, who's bad…'), and the car door slammed shut. At least she was in a good mood, he thought, jumping down into his yard.

Emily picked him up with a smile and gave him a hug. Then she held him up in front of her so he faced her. Her brow creased.

He blinked hello, purring loudly.

'Imperial Leather,' she said.

Theodore was confused.

'Carbolic soap,' she explained, pulling him closer. 'You smell of carbolic soap and...'

She inhaled deeply.

'Tuna!'

Theodore tried to wriggle free.

She held onto him tightly. 'Someone's been feeding you, haven't they?' she said. 'I wonder... Who still uses Imperial Leather?'

Theodore struggled in her grasp.

'Someone who uses carbolic soap has been feeding you tuna,' she said, her eyes wide.

There was nothing wrong with Emily's powers of deduction, thought Theodore. Perhaps he'd underestimated her, he thought, as he was dropped to the floor.

Emily slumped on the sofa. On her lap there was the mail she'd retrieved from the doormat. Two bills and one large manila envelope. She opened the bills and shook her head in dismay.

She didn't understand how she could work six days a week and still not have enough money to last until the end of the month. It was not as though she was extravagant. She did not smoke. She drank a few bottles of wine a week, but didn't everyone?

She opened the brown envelope. There was one sheet of A4 with a pink post-it note, on which her mother had written: 'Thought this might be useful.'

It was a photocopied page from a medical encyclopaedia, titled 'How to Deal with Excessive Perspiration.'

She tossed the papers onto the coffee table and stroked Theodore. She was about to text Jonathan but remembered he was working late in the office. She took the takeaway menu from the table. She took her mobile from her pocket. Theodore rubbed himself against her thigh.

'No duck for you, tuna face,' she said, dialling the number for the Lucky Twin.

Her calls were met by a computerized voice repeating 'Your call cannot be taken right now. Please try again later…'

She noticed her hands were clammy as she replaced the telephone on its cradle. She slipped her sandals back on and a few seconds later began the march over the Big Dipper to the Lucky Twin.

Pillow Talk

Theodore watched from the front window as she marched up the street; she was going to be gone some time. He exited through the cat flap and a moment later approached Wendy Morris's house.

Arthur was sitting in Theodore's preferred surveillance location, behind the trellis fence. Theodore jumped up onto the wall on the opposite side of the alley. He counted two pigeons, both perched up on the gutter. From this side of the back alley, Theodore could not see into the kitchen. He paced the wall with agitation.

At least he knew where Arthur was, he thought; now might be a good time to check up on his house and find out why Craig's telescope was pointing at the window with the blue curtains.

He jumped back down into the alley and trotted up the hill, his tail held aloft. He kept going past his own house until he was facing the house with the blue satin curtains. He glanced down the alleyway and saw in the distance Arthur's black silhouette. He was still watching the pigeons.

Theodore jumped up onto the back wall of Arthur's house. He glanced back down the hill but could not see the black cat from this position. He made his way along the boundary wall towards the house, his ears folded back, tail held straight up. He was in enemy territory.

Below him was an overgrown raised garden area that Arthur apparently used as his toilet; Theodore noted that he wasn't one to cover. The rest of the yard was concreted over. It looked like Arthur's owner did not sweep the yard often, if at all.

Theodore jumped down and began to examine a mound of brown mulch in a drain.

He fished out a feather with his paw. It might be a pigeon feather. It might be from Peter Morris's prize pigeon, Ethel, or one of the others that had disappeared. But then again it might just have blown in. He surveyed the raised garden area but didn't venture in. He would return and search the yard in more detail later, he decided.

He glanced up at the window with the blue curtains. He jumped back onto the boundary wall, then onto the felted roof of the extension. He made his way across the flat roof, then jumped up onto the bedroom windowsill.

He looked back across the yard, to the houses opposite; he wondered if Craig had his telescope trained on him at that moment.

The sash window was still open a couple of inches and from inside Theodore made out the moans and groans of human copulation. The smell of sex mixed with musky aftershave came from the room.

He edged along the windowsill and peered into the dark room. It was as he had suspected: Ahmet lay on top of Arthur's owner.

Theodore recognized the woman. She was the blue Fiat driver who had almost run him over.

Diane Banks's face was turned towards the window, her mouth parted. But in the gloom of the bedroom Theodore did not know if she was looking at him, past him or just staring into space. Meanwhile Ahmet pounded away on top of her. After a short while, the two bodies lay still. A minute later Diane lit a cigarette.

'I am worried,' Ahmet said, still catching his breath. 'Zeynep… She suspects.'

'She doesn't know anything,' Diane said, blowing out smoke.

'I tell you – she found black cat hairs in my underpants.'

'Just roller them before you go home, darling.'

'Then there was the old man,' Ahmet said. 'Peter Morris… He saw me coming out of the back gate.'

Theodore's ears pricked up at the mention of Peter.

'Big deal,' Diane said. 'He's dead. Dead men don't talk…'

'He said to me… I know what you've been up to.'

'So you killed him?' Diane laughed.

'It is not a joking matter,' Ahmet said. 'He knew… He knew about us. And if he knew, maybe he told others. He might have told his wife. You know what people are like… Zeynep must not know about us.'

Diane stubbed out her cigarette. 'Don't worry so much,' she said. 'Nobody will find out.'

'I am worried,' Ahmet said again. 'Maybe we shouldn't see each other for some time.'

'You don't mean that,' Diane said, reaching under the duvet.

'Zeynep,' Ahmet said. 'She is suspicious.'

'Don't worry about your little wife,' Diane said. She ducked under the duvet, and a minute later her head began to bob up and down.

Ahmet began to groan, his head bent into the pillow.

Theodore turned and jumped back down onto the felted flat roof of the extension; he had seen enough.

Then he noticed Arthur on the rear wall. The black cat's back was arched, his fur bristling. His baleful stare met Theodore's.

Theodore jumped down onto the boundary wall and Arthur proceeded along the back wall to cut off his escape.

The cats stopped a few feet apart.

Theodore jumped down into the yard.

Arthur jumped down too. He stood opposite Theodore. His tail swished from side to side.

Theodore retreated towards the house. He crouched down, his eyes half closed, ears flattened to the side of his head. The tip of his tail tapped the ground. Should he flee or make a stand?

Arthur advanced, growling.

Theodore growled back and arched his tail.

He turned sideways and arched his back to look bigger. His pupils dilated. His fur stood on end.

Arthur took a step towards him.

Theodore bared his teeth and hissed.

Then Arthur launched himself at Theodore.

Theodore rolled onto his back, all four legs out, claws extended. Ready. Then he kicked out with his hind legs as Arthur landed on him.

Crispy Duck Hangover

Theodore was woken by an angel. Her bright blue eyes stared into his. Her nose was a pale pink T. She was surrounded by the golden aura cast by a street light further up the back alley. She licked at his face, like his mother had once done.

As his eyes focussed, he noticed she had a tabby face. An angel with a tabby face, he thought: he must be dreaming.

He closed his eyes, trying to remember what had happened. When he opened them again, the angelic tabby-faced cat was still there, slowly coming into focus.

It's time to go home, she purred softly.

Home?

Yes. It's time that you went home, she purred. *You need to rest. You had a fight… Don't you remember?*

Of course the angel cat did not actually speak to Theodore, the way that humans do. She conveyed her meaning through purring, her eyes and the gentle movements of her tongue as it glided over his fur.

Theodore tried to raise himself from the ground but his back legs were too weak. He remembered the fight with Arthur, his back legs kicking and pushing the black cat away, not allowing his opponent the opportunity to get at his neck.

He remembered the other cat's teeth fastening on his ear, then pulling, the cartilage tearing. Arthur chewing on the gristly morsel. Then Theodore fleeing over the wall, down into the back alley. Arthur chasing him, his mouth red with Theodore's blood. Running blindly towards home. Arthur catching up. Jumping up onto a back wall. Then a mighty blow to his side and falling…

It was night but the moon was almost full. Belle the Birman cat licked his face.

How long had he been lying there?

On one side of him there was a brick wall; on the other the side of a shed. He must be in the Turkish couple's yard, he realized.

He tried to get to his feet again and this time managed, his limbs aching from the fight. He walked a few trembling yards.

There was a cat flap at the bottom of the gate. He turned and blinked goodbye to Belle before exiting into the back alley.

He staggered down the alley until he was at his own gate. He didn't have the strength to jump up onto the back wall. He miaowed at the gate hoping that Emily would hear. He waited but she didn't come. He rested and then miaowed again.

He lay on the ground in front of the gate. He could smell the safety of his own yard but couldn't enter it.

He listened to the hustle and bustle of other cats going about their business. He heard the wail of a female in heat. The rustle of leaves as another cat followed the trail of a mouse. The soft padding of a thousand paws in the night. He closed his eyes.

What had he achieved this evening besides being beaten up by a thug of a cat?

He'd discovered that a middle-aged divorcee was having an affair with a Turkish taxi driver. He'd discovered that Craig Foster liked to watch them have sexual intercourse through his telescope.

But what did any of that have to do with who killed Peter Morris and who or what was taking his pigeons?

As night began to turn to the grey of morning and the birds began to call out for the dawn to come, he stirred from his spot by the gate. He jumped up onto the top of the back wall and made his way to his back door. His whole body trembled, from his whiskers to the tip of his tail.

He paused in the kitchen. Snoring was coming from the front room.

Emily was lying on the sofa. An empty bottle of Chardonnay stood beside a wine glass on the table. Two foil trays lay on the floor. Apart from a few scraps of aromatic duck, they were empty. A tray that contained strips of spring onion and cucumber and a cellophane package of pancakes lay unopened.

Theodore ate the remains of the duck and licked the grease from the tray. Then he jumped up onto the sofa and settled on her stomach.

He kneaded the soft cushion of her belly through the damp cotton of her t-shirt and felt some peace of mind return. His heart beat slowed down. He purred as he pushed his paws into her, but Emily didn't wake. He applied his claws but she still didn't wake.

He made his way to her chest and looked at her face.

It was pallid, clammy. Her mouth was slightly open. Drool had dried white down the side of her mouth. Grease from the crispy duck was stuck in hard brown globules at the edges of her mouth.

What was wrong with her? he asked himself.

But Theodore was too tired to come up with any answers. Instead he went to sleep.

Emily woke some hours later. She glanced at the clock on the mantelpiece, then at her wristwatch.

'Pooh sticks!' she said. 'I'm going to be late… I'm going to be really late.'

She picked Theodore up from her stomach and put him on the floor. Then she swung herself round.

She glanced at the empty wine bottle on the table and then the empty tin foil containers on the floor. 'What's happening to me?' she said to herself.

I was wondering the same, Theodore thought.

'I'm going to lose my job at this rate,' she said. 'Then there's not going to be any more crispy duck.'

Maybe it's the crispy duck that's the problem.

'Life without crispy duck is not a life worth living.'

I really do think you have a crispy duck problem.

Emily turned to him. She took a quick breath. 'Oh, my God. What happened to *you*?'

Theodore remembered that he'd lost part of his ear in the fight with Arthur. A triangle was missing from the middle. The upper part of what remained was now folded down over itself. What was left of the lower part was a mess of cartilage, fur and scab.

'Pooh sticks,' Emily said again. 'I don't believe this is happening to me.' She picked Theodore up. 'We're going to the vet's.'

Emily carried him through to the dining room and got the cat carrier out from the under-stairs cupboard.

At least wash your face before we go, Theodore complained, as he was pushed into the plastic box.

Human Indiscretions

Theodore was sitting on the sofa next to Emily, who was eating crispy duck from a silver tray. She used her fingers to push the meat into her mouth while watching a television programme about a grizzly-faced chef trying to turn around failing restaurants. Theodore waited his turn, trying not to drool.

He heard Jonathan's footsteps on the pavement outside. Then there were his familiar three sharp knocks on the door.

Emily pushed the foil tray back into the plastic bag, tied the bag up and rushed outside to dispose of it. A minute later she opened the front door, her hands wet. 'I wasn't expecting you so early,' she said, wiping grease from her chin with the back of a hand.

'I got off work early for once,' Jonathan said. 'Thought I'd surprise you.' He walked into the house and bent down to give her a kiss. 'I thought you were cutting back on the Chinese,' he said wiping grease from his own mouth.

'I'm trying,' Emily said. 'It's difficult. I relapsed...' She laughed.

Theodore exited the cat flap. In the yard he circled the bin. It was galvanized steel and even if he managed to push it over, it would make such a clatter, Emily would be out of the house in seconds.

Grey cloud gathered over the yard.

He felt cheated. Life would be so much better if Jonathan wasn't around. He schemed silently, dreaming up ways of annoying the intruder to the point he would give up on Emily and find someone without the complications. Someone without a cat...

People want a simple life, Theodore philosophized. *They just don't realize it.*

'I wish I could lie in bed all day,' Emily had told him on more than one occasion.

Well, why don't you? Theodore thought back.

All this rushing around, sitting in cars in traffic jams, going to jobs that you don't even like, just so you have the money to pay for the fuel to get to work and the sandwich you cram into your mouth in the ten minute lunch break (if you're lucky), and then driving home, where you fritter away your money online on products which you don't need. People needed to do less, Theodore concluded; they just didn't realize it.

As long as he continued to annoy Jonathan, Theodore reasoned, it was only a matter of time until he signed back on that dating website and found someone else. Then it would be Theodore and Emily again. It was only a matter of time.

He returned inside. Jonathan's rucksack was at the foot of the stairs. Evidently he was planning to stay over.

Theodore raised his rear end and shot a jet of urine over the bag. Then he went outside again.

On the table in front of the back window, Michael had lit candles. In the kitchen Theodore watched as Michael tapped purplish red steaks with his little wooden mallet.

It was Philip's birthday and Michael was cooking him a special meal. Philip's present was waiting on the table. A cube wrapped carefully in pink crepe paper.

Philip walked in. 'Bit dark in here,' he said, flicking on the lights.

Michael walked over to the table and blew out the candles, sending wisps of smoke into the air.

'Oh, candles,' Philip said. 'I didn't realize. Sorry.'

'Never mind,' Michael said. 'I got you a little present.'

Philip tore open the cube. 'A new watch,' he said, his voice not trying to hide his disappointment. He opened the box and removed the grey Swatch. 'I really wanted a Rolex,' he said, putting the watch back in its display case.

'It will go with your shirt,' Michael said. 'The shirt I bought you last week. Grey's all the rage at the moment…'

Philip shrugged. 'If you say so,' he said.

Theodore yawned. Why Michael put up with Philip was beyond his comprehension. He jumped down into the alley and then back up the other side, on top of Wendy Morris's wall.

Wendy and Irene had just finished dinner.

'I never knew you were keen on pizza,' he heard Irene say.

'Peter never liked foreign food,' Wendy said. 'He would never try anything new. Now he's not here, I thought I'd have a go at something a bit different.'

'Well, I've had a few pizzas in my time,' Irene went on, 'but roast beef and peas are new toppings on me.' She laughed.

'Just using up a few bits,' Wendy said.

She took their plates over to the kitchen sink and dumped them into the water.

Zeynep entered the alley further up the hill. She began shouting for her cat. She walked down the alley, a thin coat buttoned over her bulging belly.

She hadn't yet given up on Bal, Theodore realized. He jumped down from the wall and followed behind Zeynep. They exited the access alley and out onto the next street.

Zeynep paused on the pavement, in front of Diane's house. A taxi was parked outside. Ahmet's taxi.

She took her mobile phone from her coat pocket. She pressed the touch screen and then held the phone to her ear.

A moment later a faint tune could be heard from within the house. Zeynep thrust the mobile phone back into her pocket. She marched back into the alley. She didn't stop until she reached her own gate.

Theodore followed her as far as her yard. He took up a position on the back wall. He spied Belle sitting on the kitchen table.

Zeynep went straight up to the back bedroom. She swept the unfinished Ottoman dolls house from the table with her forearm. She stamped on its roof. She grabbed the shoebox and emptied its contents onto the floor.

'Pervert! she screamed, spying a pair of her black lace knickers.

She pulled the completed models from the shelves around the room and stamped on them, balsa wood crumpling beneath her shoes.

She came back downstairs and paced the kitchen. She took her mobile phone from her pocket again and began to jab at the screen.

She pressed the phone to her ear.

'Hello… Yes… Police…,' she said.

A few seconds went by.

'Hello. Yes… Is that the police? Yes.'

Another silence and then: 'I have information about the Clementhorpe murder… My husband. He was very late coming home that night… And when he did, he washed his clothing… It is very unlike him to wash his own clothes. Especially late at night…'

Theodore's ears twitched.

'I think he is acting differently since what happened… His name? It is Ahmet. Ahmet Akbulut. He works for Crow Line taxis.'

There was a pause.

Then: 'He is at work now. Crow Line taxis. His car is white. A white Toyota Avensis.

And then: 'You should know he has a temper.'

Theodore's brow furrowed. *Ahmet? A liar and a cheat perhaps, but a murderer?*

He jumped down from the wall and trotted back round to where Ahmet's taxi was parked in front of Diane's house.

He sat below the still warm engine and waited for the police to arrive. He didn't have to wait long.

Le Morte d'Arthur

Theodore entered the front room to be faced by two large orange-furred feline monsters. They stood their ground in the middle of the room, staring at Theodore with wide eyes.

I'll take you both on, Theodore cried, throwing himself into the melee. I'll knock the stuffing out of you!

He singled one of them out, jumped onto its stomach and began working with his hind legs, digging into and ripping at its soft underbelly. Orange fur flew up into the air.

We'll see who's tough, he panted.

His opponent soon gave up the struggle and submitted to Theodore's superior strength. He turned to the other, who had stood waiting its turn.

Now for you.

Theodore flew at him, sending them both skidding across the floor.

When they came to rest, Theodore was on top. He went for the other's throat. He dug his teeth into the soft of the neck and took hold with his teeth. He shook his head from side to side, his jaw clamped shut. He pulled away and spat out the contents of his mouth. He sank his fangs in again, tugging at what lay beneath his enemy's chin, his back legs working at the other's soft belly. When he'd finished with him, he surveyed the scene.

Orange synthetic fur and yellow foam lay scattered across the floor. The eyes of one of his enemies flicked open, then closed, never to open again.

'My slippers!' Emily cried, coming into the front room to see what the racket was about. 'What have you done to my slippers, Theo? They're ruined.'

Theodore slunk past her into the hallway, his tail held low.

'Theo!' Emily called after him.

He made his way into the kitchen and exited the cat flap.

'Theodore!' Emily shouted from inside, but he was already up on the back wall and on his way to Wendy's.

The police had knocked on Diane's door following Zeynep's phone call and had taken Ahmet back to Fulford Police Station for questioning. They had kept him in custody overnight. In the morning they'd collected Zeynep and then shortly afterwards Diane.

'I was out with Rocky,' Irene said. 'Diane was still wearing her nightgown when they took her away. They must have got her out of bed…'

'You'd have thought they'd have let her get dressed,' Wendy said.

'I wonder what she has to do with it,' Irene said.

'She had a thing for that taxi driver,' Wendy said. 'Peter told me about them. He'd seen him coming out of her back gate one evening.'

'Did he now? They took away some bin bags from the Turkish couple's. I reckon they were his clothes. Evidence, you know.'

'But why would he want to harm Peter?' Wendy asked. 'They didn't even know each other.' She was standing in front of the kitchen window, rolling out dough. Her navy blue apron was grey across her bosom from decades of flour and grease. She'd had her greying hair dyed red that morning. It looked more carroty than she'd hoped.

'There must be something in it,' Irene said. 'They wouldn't have taken him in for no reason now, would they?'

'No, I suppose not.'

Wendy laid the dough into a pie dish and thumbed the edges.

'But why would he want to harm Peter?' she said again.

From the back wall of Wendy's yard, Theodore also pondered this question. Peter Morris had known that Ahmet was sleeping with Diane. Had Ahmet killed Peter Morris because he knew about the affair? He could have used the pretext of asking after the missing cat, and when Peter had opened the gate, Ahmet had clobbered him.

Theodore looked across at the pigeon loft. One solitary bird perched on its roof. He inspected the sky for its companions but there was none. He turned his attention back to the kitchen window and saw Wendy washing dishes at the kitchen sink.

'Have you heard from Laura?' Irene asked. 'Since the funeral.'

'No,' Wendy said. 'Not a peep.'

'Such a shame,' Irene said. 'If I were you, I'd be round there. He's your grandchild, you know.'

'It's all because of what happened between her and Peter… They never saw eye to eye… But Peter was set in his ways. He had his opinions and he stuck to them.'

'I know that,' Irene said bluntly. 'But Peter's not around anymore. You have a chance to set things right. You have a beautiful grandson. You don't want to miss out on that…'

Then Theodore sensed another animal approach. He turned to see Arthur padding along the back alley, his tail up straight. The black cat stopped directly below Theodore and miaowed up at him. It was an order: 'Get out of the way or else!'

Theodore backed away, further down the wall.

Garfield slippers were one thing. Arthur was another.

Arthur jumped up onto the wall and took up Theodore's spot, behind the barbed wire topped trellis that surrounded the Morris's yard. He hadn't eaten that morning. Diane had been whisked off to the police station to be interviewed before she'd had chance to feed him.

Theodore watched as he eyed the last remaining pigeon, the tip of his tongue showing.

He doesn't have a chance, Theodore thought, watching as Arthur paced backwards and forwards, up and down the length of wall.

The eighteen inch high trellis was fixed in the middle of the wall, a slight gap on either side. Arthur paced on the outside of the trellis. He went beyond the Morris's yard, towards Theodore, who retreated further along the wall.

Then Arthur began to run towards Wendy Morris's yard. When he reached the trellis he jumped two feet into the air before landing on the inside of the trellis, three yards further along.

Theodore blinked in astonishment. Arthur was inside the Morris's yard.

The black cat stalked up and down along the wall, his eyes fixed on the pigeon, his ears folded flat.

The pigeon launched itself into the air and flapped about the yard. It was making for the safety of the loft when Arthur jumped. They met in mid-air. Arthur's teeth sunk into the bird's nape. By the time they hit the ground, the bird was dead. Arthur shook it for good measure.

He turned around, the bird held firmly in his mouth, looking for an escape.

The stepladder Peter Morris had used to clean out the pigeon loft was leant against the back wall. Arthur was soon up the ladder and back on top of the wall, the dead pigeon clasped in his mouth. He paced along the wall once more. Then, breaking into a run, he jumped into the air.

Then Theodore saw Wendy Morris out in her yard, rolling pin in hand. She raised the wooden cylinder, then threw it.

It flipped through the air before cracking Arthur's skull.

Arthur landed in the back alley with a soft thud. The pigeon dropped a few feet away. The rolling pin landed a moment later.

Theodore saw a small pool of blood begin to form on the cobbles around Arthur's head. He heard a bolt being pulled and then slippered steps across the cobblestones.

He hurried further along the wall seeking the cover of an overgrown privet hedge. When he turned, he saw Wendy leaning over the dead cat.

She picked him up and carried him at arm's length into her yard. Arthur hung limp. A moment later she returned with a sheet of newspaper for the pigeon.

Theodore listened as the back gate was bolted behind her. He looked up and down the back alley. There was no one... No one to have witnessed the felinicide.

He approached Wendy's yard, stopping short of the trellis. He glanced at the splash of blood on the cobbles and the few flecks from the pigeon a few feet away.

Theodore had not been friends with Arthur but he would never wish such a brutal end to one of his own kind.

Arthur had been acting in accordance with his baser instinct. He hadn't been fed that morning. He'd been hungry. Food had presented itself in the form of a pigeon. He had risked his life in killing the bird and, as a result, he was dead. Arthur had taken a gamble, Theodore thought, and had lost. He had paid the price with his life.

Theodore looked down into the yard. Arthur lay on the concrete beneath the pigeon loft. On the chimney of the Morris house a crow cawed out the death.

Wendy was in the outbuilding. She came out with a bucket and mop.

Irene was standing by the back door. 'I can't believe you've gone and killed Diane's cat,' she said, clucking her tongue.

'Well, I did,' Wendy said. 'It had one of his birds.'

'But you killed Diane's cat...'

Wendy pushed past Irene and filled the bucket at the kitchen sink.

'Those cats are always killing things,' she said.

'Diane thought the world of that cat,' Irene said.

'I didn't *mean* to kill him,' Wendy said. 'I only meant to scare him off.'

She turned off the kitchen tap. She went out the back door carrying her plastic bucket of soapy water.

Irene followed. 'I'd better be getting along,' she said. 'I need to take Rocky out for his walk.'

'Don't you go telling to Diane about this,' Wendy said.

Irene didn't respond. She hurried down the back alley to her own gate.

Theodore watched as Wendy washed the cobbles of blood.

Then she went back inside her house. She took a bin bag from a kitchen drawer. She came outside again and pushed Arthur's body inside the bin bag. Then she went back inside.

A few minutes later Theodore watched as Wendy Morris pulled her shopping trolley along the back alley.

Theodore looked back down into the yard. There was a dark stain where Arthur had been. He jumped down into the alley. He raced out into the street. He spied Wendy, her shopping trolley bumping along behind her, as she turned onto Scarcroft Road. Then she disappeared from sight.

He raced down Alcuin Terrace and spotted Wendy hurrying along the road. Then she disappeared.

When he arrived at the spot where she'd disappeared, he noticed a gate set into the hedge. He ducked under and began to pad along the path that extended up through the allotments.

Wendy was further up the path, dragging the shopping trolley along behind her over the rough ground.

Theodore trotted behind, keeping to the sides of the path. Several times she glanced behind her but Theodore darted into the undergrowth.

Wendy stopped in a small clearing beside a large mound of decomposing grass clippings. Theodore watched as she undid a zip and took from her shopping trolley the black bin bag. She made a hole in the brown mulch and pushed the bag inside. Then she pushed the moulding grass back over. A moment later she continued along the path, over Scarcroft Hill towards the Knavesmire.

Theodore approached the mound. He inspected the place where she'd replaced the brown grass. Then he dug out the grass with his front paws, sending it flying behind him. He soon exposed the black bin liner. With a claw he split the thin black plastic.

A lifeless amber eye stared back at him.

The Allotments

Jonathan was watching television while Emily was upstairs having a bath.

Suddenly Theodore darted in, carrying a plastic bag in his mouth. He rolled over, wrapping the bag around himself.

'What an earth are you up to?' Jonathan said, removing his feet from the table. 'Don't you know it's dangerous to play with plastic bags?'

Theodore rolled onto his back, paws in the air, the plastic bag below him.

Arthur's been killed by Wendy, wrapped in a bin liner and buried in the allotments, he wanted to say.

Jonathan lent over. He pulled the plastic bag from beneath the cat. 'You want your tummy tickling, Theo?' he said, digging his fingers into Theodore's stomach.

Theodore got to his feet and exited the front room.

Jonathan put his feet back up on the coffee table and tried to watch his programme again. But a minute later he heard a miaow from outside. He stood up and went over to the front window. He saw Theodore sitting on the front wall. He returned to the sofa, determined to watch his programme.

Theodore miaowed again. He miaowed as loudly as he could. It was some minutes before Jonathan's face appeared again at the window.

He jumped down and marched into the middle of the road. He stretched out on the warm tarmac. It was not a busy street but it wouldn't be too long before a car came.

He heard Jonathan shouting up to the bathroom: 'Your cat's in the road.'

93

Theodore did not hear Emily's muffled response, but a moment later the front door opened and Jonathan appeared, shaking his head.

Theodore stood up and began to walk down the middle of the street, between the parked cars, his tail held up behind him.

'Do you have a death wish?' Jonathan asked Theodore's retreating fluffy rear end.

He began to follow Theodore down the middle of Avondale Terrace, calling his name. He broke into a short sprint in an attempt to grab him, but Theodore was too quick for him.

Theodore turned left at the bottom of the street and waited for Jonathan to catch up with him. As soon as he saw Jonathan rounding the corner, he trotted ahead, turning every once in a while to make sure he was still being followed.

Twenty minutes later Theodore led Jonathan back to the house. In his arms he carried Arthur, still wrapped in the bin liner.

The front door had been left open while they'd been gone. Emily now stood in the doorway, her wet hair tied back.

'Where have you two been?' she said. 'I was worried.'

'Scarcroft Allotments,' Jonathan said. 'Theodore wanted to show me something.'

He held up the black bag and grimaced.

'What is it?'

He opened the bag to show her the dead cat. 'It looks like he's been whacked over the head,' he said, pointing to the black fur matted with blood.

Theodore circled his legs. He's not so stupid after all, he thought.

'Why have you brought a dead cat in here?' Emily suddenly shouted. 'If you think you are going to bring that thing into my house, you've got another thing coming.'

'But your cat led me to it,' he said. 'I think someone's killed it.'

'I don't want a dead cat in my house!'

'I found it in the allotments,' Jonathan went on. 'It doesn't have a collar… Somebody must have killed it and hid it in the allotments.'

'Don't be stupid,' Emily said, hands on hips. 'It'll have been knocked down by a car and crawled into the allotments to die. Cats do that…'

'But it was in a bin liner.'

'Maybe the car driver put it in a bin liner and hid it in the allotments rather than owning up to it… I just don't want a dead cat in my house.'

'Well,' Jonathan said, holding the bag out in front of him, 'what do you suggest I do with it?'

'I don't care what you do with it. Just get it out of here.'

The black cat Jonathan had found in the allotments had reminded him of his own cat that had died the year before. Perhaps that was why he had not hesitated to pick it up. He didn't mention this to Emily. He shook his head.

Theodore stared up at him. What are you going to do now? his eyes asked.

'I'll take it back to mine and bury it,' Jonathan said, matter-of-factly. 'I'll be back later and then we can go out and get something to eat.'

'Sounds like a plan,' Emily said. 'It'll give me time to dry my hair.'

As soon as the front door had closed behind Jonathan, Emily went upstairs, and Theodore heard the whir of the hairdryer. He padded through the dining room and back out into the yard.

He jumped onto the back wall of his yard and looked down into the alley. The blue cobbles looked polished where Wendy had washed them of blood. He pondered the scene a moment. The rolling pin!

Wendy had removed the dead cat. She had come back for the pigeon. But what had happened to the rolling pin?

He replayed Arthur's last seconds. The moment the rolling pin hit Arthur's head with a crack. Wood on bone. Arthur hitting the ground with a soft thud. The hollow sound of the rolling pin landing and then another hollow noise as it bounced off down the alley.

The rolling pin had bounced, then rolled down the hill, Theodore concluded.

He looked down the alley. The rolling pin was nowhere to be seen. He jumped down.

Each house had a gate recessed into the back wall. The rolling pin must have rolled down the hill and come to rest against a gate.

Theodore trotted down the alley, inspecting each gateway in turn. He was almost at the bottom when he spotted the rolling pin lying flush against a gate.

With his front paws he rolled it back out into the middle of the alley and then up the hill towards home. Murderers always miss something, he reflected, as he patted the rolling pin up the hill.

The rolling pin was still dotted with flour. He noted some specks of dark red. Theodore smiled to himself. He had all the proof he needed. Emily surely would be able to put two and two together.

He arrived at his back gate. He rolled the rolling pin up against it. He miaowed. He could hear Emily's hairdryer whirring from upstairs. He miaowed again.

He heard a backdoor open down the alley. A loose pane of glass rattled in its frame as the door closed. It was Wendy's backdoor.

The hair dryer stopped. Theodore miaowed.

He heard steps on the stairs. A moment later the kitchen door was opened. At the same time the bolt of Wendy's back gate was pulled back.

Murderers always returned to the scene of the crime, Theodore remembered, his front paws still holding the rolling pin up against his gate.

He pulled the rolling pin back towards him, then against the gate as hard as he could.

He heard steps coming towards him from inside his yard. He heard steps coming towards him from down the hill.

'Is that you Theodore?' he heard Emily say.

He miaowed back. *Let me in.*

'Why can't you just jump over the wall?' she said. 'You usually do.'

The bolt was pulled back and the gate swung open.

Theodore pushed the rolling pin into the safety of his yard, then followed after.

'What's this?' Emily asked, picking up the rolling pin.

'It's mine,' Wendy Morris said.

Theodore looked on as Emily handed the rolling pin to Wendy.

'I've been looking for it all over,' Wendy said.

'I just opened my gate and there it was,' Emily said, smiling nervously.

'I heard him miaowing in the alley,' Wendy went on. 'And when I came out to see what the matter was, I saw him with it.'

'He's always bringing things in.'

'Yes,' Wendy said, smiling. 'I suppose he is.'

Emily thought of the pigeon feathers Theodore had dropped on her pillow. 'Well, I'm glad Theodore managed to find your rolling pin,' she said.

'Goodness knows how it came to be in the back alley,' Wendy said.

Emily noticed that Wendy had had her hair dyed red and had lost several pounds since she had last seen her.

'Are you managing all right?' she asked.

'I'm coping,' Wendy said. 'What else do you do?'

'If I can do anything?'

Emily felt Theodore rubbing against her calves. She remembered that she still had to paint her toenails. 'Well, I'm glad you got your rolling pin back.'

Wendy said, 'I would have been lost without it.' She bent down and reached out to pat Theodore.

Theodore backed away and hissed up at her.

'Theodore!' Emily said.

'Not to worry,' Wendy said. 'I'd better be off. I've got a pie in the oven.'

Emily stood in the gateway and watched as Wendy marched back down the hill, rolling pin in hand. She shut the gate, scooped Theodore up and pressed him to her.

'What am I going to do with you?' she said. 'Stealing people's rolling pins… Whatever next?'

She carried him upstairs and placed him on the bed while she painted her toenails.

Jonathan returned with two plastic bags. One contained two bottles of Pinot Grigio from the little supermarket round the corner. The other was from the Lucky Twin takeaway.

'What have you got there?' Emily asked.

'Some wine and a Chinese,' Jonathan said.

'Crispy duck?'

'Crispy duck for you.'

'You know I'm trying to cut down on Chinese food,' Emily said, grinning.

'Well, I didn't fancy going into town now,' Jonathan said. 'So I thought I'd pick up a takeaway while I was passing. I thought I'd go for the fish and chip special…'

As they ate the Chinese takeaway, drank the Italian wine and watched an American film, Emily asked Jonathan if he had buried the cat.

Jonathan said that he hadn't. He had intended to, but on his way home he'd passed a green wheelie bin left conveniently next to the footpath and had dropped the dead cat inside.

'You put the cat in a wheelie bin?'

Emily, who was on her second glass of wine, began to giggle.

'It was *dead*,' Jonathan said. 'I don't see that it really matters.'

'Was it empty… the wheelie bin?' Emily asked, laughing.

'Yes.'

'Well, it's going to be a fortnight until it gets buried now.'

Jonathan laughed too. He had a drink of wine and then picked at his fish. The batter was almost orange. He took a forkful of the white meat from under the batter and chewed. It didn't taste of fish. Chicken maybe, but definitely not fish.

Theodore rubbed against his legs. A small pool of drool had begun to form on the laminate floor. Jonathan handed him a chunk of fish/chicken.

'I think I've found the way to your cat's heart,' he told Emily, watching Theodore wolf down the morsel.

'Yes,' Emily said nodding, her mouth full of duck. 'He seems to like that special fish.'

Jonathan handed him another chunk, then another. Theodore purred, chewing on the fish, his mouth agape, drool sliding down his chin.

Theodore was woken in the night by his stomach. It growled angrily.

He got to his paws, jumped down onto the floor and headed for the door. His intention was to get out to the yard and his litter tray as fast as possible and relieve himself of whatever foul mixture was brewing inside.

The door had been pulled too though, and before Theodore could nose it open, his bottom spurted out a jet of diarrhoea.

He spun round in surprise, sending a line of brownish orange across the bookcase, splattering the broken spines of a dozen Sidney Sheldons. Once started, Theodore had no option but to let his lower body continue. A lower shelf of well-thumbed James Pattersons met the same fate.

When it was over, Theodore surveyed the damage. Three shelves of books were ruined. He imagined Emily the next morning shoving her paperback library into bin liners, cursing the unwitting feline literary critic.

He turned around and something caught his eye. In the corner, by the foot of the sofa, Jonathan's dinner plate had been left until the morning. On the plate, the crispy fish shell pulsed orange in the darkness.

Surprise Pie

Saturday morning, as Emily and Jonathan lay in bed, there was a knock at the door.

'Can you get that?' Emily said. 'I'm expecting a parcel.'

Jonathan got out of bed and hurried downstairs, Theodore following at his heels. When he opened the front door, there was no parcel but a woman with short dark hair standing on the doorstep.

Theodore eyed her from behind Jonathan's. It was the woman who had almost run him over. Arthur's owner and Ahmet's lover Diane.

'Can I help?' Jonathan asked, rubbing his eyes.

'You haven't seen a black cat, have you?' Diane asked. 'He hasn't had his breakfast this morning. He never misses his breakfast. And he didn't come home last night. I think something might have happened to him... He answers to Arthur... I was wondering if you could check your shed. Make sure he hasn't got in.'

Jonathan's brain had yet to awake fully. Rather than telling Diane that he hadn't seen her cat and promising to check the shed, he told her the truth.

'I'm afraid your cat's dead,' he said.

'Dead?' Diane opened her mouth to show a piece of white chewing gum.

'Yes. I found him in the allotments. I think he'd been hit...'

'Hit? Hit by a car?'

Jonathan paused. His head pounded. 'Yes,' he said. 'He'd been hit by a car. He must have dragged himself into the allotments.'

He didn't tell her about Theodore leading him to the compost heap or the bin liner in which he'd been buried.

Instead he said, 'Yes, he'd been hit by a car. I didn't want to leave him there in the allotments, so I brought him back here.'

Diane began to cry. She wiped tears from her reddened cheeks. She chewed vigorously on her chewing gum, taking it all in.

'I can't believe it,' she said.

'I went and buried him,' Jonathan went on. Lying was easy, he thought, once you got going. 'In my garden…'

'That was thoughtful,' she said, sniffing. 'Can I see?'

'He's not here,' Jonathan said. 'You see I don't live here… This is my girlfriend's house. She doesn't have a garden. So I took the cat back to my house and buried him there… Under a tree.'

'Under a tree?' Diane said. A tear ran down her cheek at this minor detail. She blew her nose noisily.

They stood staring at each a minute.

'Could I visit his grave?'

Jonathan looked down at his tartan pyjama bottoms and wrinkled Ramones t-shirt. He noted a dried smear of grease across his chest. He felt Theodore's tail against his ankle. He wanted to scratch the place but restrained himself. 'I'm not really dressed at the moment,' he said.

'Perhaps later then?' Diane said, wiping a tear from her cheek. 'I believe closure is important.'

'Yes, of course,' Jonathan said warily. 'Closure… of course.'

'This afternoon?'

'I'll write down my address.'

He left Diane at the front door while he went inside and scribbled his address on a scrap of paper.

'Say two o'clock,' he said, handing over his address.

'See you at two,' Diane said, smiling, her eyes red lined and bleary.

Jonathan shut the front door and, passing the door to the front room, he stopped. There was a horrible smell coming from behind the door. He pushed the door open and saw the bookcase. He closed the door and went into the kitchen. He made himself a coffee and a tea for Emily.

When he returned upstairs, Theodore had stolen his side of the bed. He lifted him up, placed him at the bottom of the bed and climbed back in.

He explained to Emily that a woman called Diane was going to go to his house to pay her respects at her cat's grave.

'But you put it in a wheelie bin,' Emily said, sitting up and slurping her tea.

'I think it was that woman who nearly ran Theo over that time,' Jonathan said.

'She did say that she had a cat,' Emily said. 'What are you going to do?'

'I'll sort something out,' Jonathan said. 'And your cat has had an accident on your books. I reckon it was that fish that disagreed with him.'

Mid-morning, after Emily had disposed of her ruined books, wiped clean the ones which were salvageable and disinfected the bookcase, there was another knock on the door. This time Emily got it. It was the parcel that she'd been expecting. 'Theo!' she called. 'I have a present for you.'

Theodore jumped down from the chest in the front room and went through to the dining room.

Emily had opened the package by the time Theodore arrived on the scene. He jumped up onto the dining room table.

Inside the package there was a tracking device. She fixed it to Theodore's purple collar.

Jonathan put down his newspaper and began reading the instructions.

Soon he had managed to set the handset to recognize the tracker. 'I don't know why you feel the need for this,' he said. 'It's not as if he's always disappearing.'

'I want to know where he gets to,' Emily said. 'He's always going off these days. Didn't he take you on a trip to the allotments yesterday? And there's cats going missing around here...'

She pressed a button on the handset and the pendant sitting on the crown of Theodore's chest began to flash red.

'I don't know what I'd do if anything happened to Theo,' she said.

After Jonathan had gone back to his own house to shower, get changed and prepare Arthur's grave, there was another knock at the Emily's door.

This time it was Wendy. Her carrot red hair was tied back. She'd coated her lips with red lipstick that morning and was wearing blue jeans and a baggy red blouse. In her hands she held out a pie.

She handed it to Emily, saying with a smile: 'A little thank you for finding my rolling pin.'

Emily took the pie and said, 'Thank you… But you really didn't need to.'

'I still cook for two,' Wendy said. 'And now's there's just the one of me. I have a freezer full of food that I'm never going to get through!'

'It looks tasty,' Emily said. 'We'll have it for dinner tomorrow.'

'I'll be off then.'

'Thanks again.'

Emily carried the pie through to the kitchen and slid it onto an empty shelf in the fridge. She closed the door and then realized she had not asked what was in the pie.

Oh, well, she thought. It'll be a surprise… A surprise pie!

Fake Funeral

Shortly after two o'clock that afternoon, there was a knock at the front door of No.8 Carsen Terrace. When Jonathan opened it, there was Diane in a black blouse and skirt. She held a posy of yellow pansies. She chewed mechanically on a piece of gum.

Jonathan suddenly felt underdressed for the occasion in his white t-shirt and jeans. He invited her in and told her to go through to the yard.

'Quite the bachelor's den you've got here,' she commented, as she walked through the front room.

Jonathan glanced about the room. He noticed the pizza box lying on the sofa, the remains of a pepperoni pizza peeping out.

'Not quite,' he said, wishing he'd tidied up.

He followed her through to the back door, noticing her black skirt stopped short of her knees.

In the yard there was a small garden area against the back wall. A red-leaved dwarf sycamore grew in the corner. A rectangle of soil under the sycamore had been recently turned over. As an added touch, Jonathan had tied two lollipop sticks into a cross using green twine and planted it at one end of the turned over patch.

Diane removed her gum from her mouth and held it between thumb and forefinger. She stood before the mock grave, her back to Jonathan. She bent down and placed the pansies onto the recently turned over soil. 'I will miss you, dear Arthur,' she said.

Jonathan backed away. 'Maybe I should leave you alone for a minute,' he said.

She turned to face him.

Charcoal rivulets of mascara had streaked down her cheeks. Her bleary eyes looked into his. 'It's just so horrible,' she said.

'I just can't believe that Arthur's there. Under the ground… In the soil.'

'No?'

'I just can't believe that he's dead and never coming back.'

'He's definitely dead and not coming back,' Jonathan said.

Diane cried harder.

Jonathan approached. He put his arms around her, and Diane turned and sobbed onto his chest.

He looked over at the back windows of the houses opposite. He felt Diane's face pressing against him, her hot tears piercing his thin cotton t-shirt, her hot breath against his chest. Her breasts pushed against his abdomen through her thin silk blouse. He felt her hands wrapping around his lower back. Her hands slipped down. He took a step backwards and she took a step forwards.

'Diane,' he said.

'Yes?'

She looked up at him, her eyes glazed, her mouth parted.

'I don't think this is really appropriate,' Jonathan said.

He felt her hands squeezing his bottom, her body pushing against him.

'I have a girlfriend,' he said.

'I know,' she said. 'But I'm not going to tell.'

'That's not the point,' Jonathan said, trying to pull away.

'You don't remember me, do you?' Diane said. 'I was the one who nearly ran over your cat. Then you find my cat run over. That's some coincidence, isn't it?'

'A coincidence, I suppose.'

'We are connected,' Diane said, pushing into him. 'Don't you see we are connected?'

'I just don't find you attractive,' Jonathan said.

Diane took a step backwards. 'She's just a silly girl,' Diane said. 'Driving around in her bloody Beetle. You can do better than that.'

Jonathan shook his head. 'I think you should say goodbye to your cat and leave.'

'I thought you were different,' Diane said. 'But you're just *boring*.'

'Let yourself out when you've done with your *closure*,' Jonathan said.

He turned and walked back into his house.

His t-shirt was sodden with Diane's tears and smudged with mascara and lipstick. He pulled it over his head and fed it into the washing machine. He turned and locked the door before going to have his second shower of the day.

Theodore peered down at Diane from between the branches of the little sycamore tree.

Although Jonathan had replaced the insoles in his boots following their first encounter, Theodore's scent had impregnated the boots, and every time he had walked from his house to Emily's and back again, he had reinforced the trail which Theodore had followed that afternoon across South Bank.

Diane stood in front of the mock grave. She dabbed at her face with the cuffs of her blouse.

She thought of Ahmet. She was still angry with him for telling the police about them.

She looked down at her cat's grave once more. Then she took a step towards the gate.

Something grey caught her eye. She looked up and saw a pair of green eyes looking down at her from between the leafy limbs of the sycamore. She took a step towards the tree and made out a grey cat sitting on a branch.

Theodore stared back at her.

'What do you think you're looking at?' she said, not expecting a response.

Theodore met her stare. His eyes bore into hers.

'It was just a wind up,' Diane said. 'Just a bit of fun.'

Theodore continued to stare at her.

'Who do you think you are to judge me? If you must know, my husband ran off with his secretary. Ten years younger than me… I was left with nothing… Only Arthur. And I had to fight to keep him… Now he's gone too. I've got nothing.

'Nothing… I might as well move back to Lancashire,' she said with an air of finality.

You might as well, thought back Theodore.

Diane wiped a fresh tear from her cheek. Then she bent down and grabbed a handful of soil and threw it at Theodore.

'Sod off!' she cried.

But Theodore was already on the other side of the wall.

'That's right... You run home!' she shouted after him.

The sound of water from the bathroom had stopped.

Diane wiped her hands on her skirt.

'Goodbye Arthur,' she said sniffing.

Then she opened the gate and, entering the alley, slammed it shut behind her.

Turkey Drumsticks, Chinese Chips and Thrush

'What's in the pie?' Jonathan asked, chewing on a piece of chewy meat.

It was Sunday evening. Emily had warmed the pie that Wendy had given her. She examined the reddish brown piece of meat at the end of her fork. 'It's certainly not chicken,' she said.

'I know that,' Jonathan said, still chewing on the same piece of meat. 'It's a bit tough…'

'Wendy gave it to us… Theodore found her rolling pin. She wanted to thank us. So she gave us this pie. I forgot to ask what was in it.'

'It's a bit tough,' Jonathan repeated.

'It's different,' Emily said, poking pieces of food around her plate.

They both ate in silence for a couple of minutes.

Then Emily put down her knife and fork and stood up. 'Where is Theo?' she said. 'I'm surprised he's not sniffing about when there's food about.'

She took the remote control for the tracker from the side and turned it on. She went into each room carrying the tracker in front of her. Returning to the dining room, she said, 'I'm not sure this tracker thing is working.'

'When was the last time you saw him?'

'Come to think of it, I'm not sure I've seen him since this morning.'

She hurried out of the back door and made a quick inspection of the yard.

'He's not out here,' she shouted back at the house.

Jonathan joined her in the backyard as she struggled with the bolt to the gate.

Once in the back alley, she consulted the tracker's remote control again, pointing it up and down the alley.

'I've got something,' she said. Two, three, four LEDs lit up. 'He's this way.'

'There he is,' Jonathan said, pointing. 'He's up on top of Wendy's wall.'

'Come here, Theodore,' Emily called. 'Come to Mummy!'

The pendant sitting on the crown of Theodore's chest was blinking frantically and the little device was emitting a series of beeps. His cover was blown... Theodore turned his back to the pair.

'He'll come home when he's ready,' Jonathan said. 'At least we know the tracker works... Let's get back to our dinner.'

'All right,' Emily said. 'But I don't like that pie. I might put a pizza in the oven.'

'Pepperoni?'

'Yes. I think I've got one in the freezer,' Emily said.

Theodore watched as they walked away. Then he turned his attention back to Wendy's kitchen window.

Wendy and Irene were sitting at the kitchen table. Wendy held a turkey drumstick in her hand and was working her way round it. Irene was forking chips into her mouth.

'One pound forty nine pence,' Wendy said.

'That's not bad,' Irene said. She trimmed some meat from the bone with her knife and fork, her head bent over her meal. 'Not bad at all. They've got a lot of meat on them.'

Wendy took a gulp of tea. 'The chips are all right too, aren't they?' she said. 'Quite tasty.'

'Yes. Not bad at all. You can't beat Mr White for chips.'

'These chips aren't from Frank's,' Wendy said with a curt smile.

'No?'

'No. I bought them from the Chinese, the Lucky Twin... Thought I'd give it a go. They were five pence cheaper...'

'I don't believe you,' Irene said, poking at the greasy yellow chips.

'Go and look in the bin if you don't believe me.'

Irene went over to the bin in the corner. She pressed down the pedal with her foot. The top flipped open to expose a brown polystyrene tray.

'I can't believe you've gone and bought your chips from the Chinese. You know as well as me that Frank White is struggling.'

'You're just annoyed that you couldn't tell the difference.'

'I am not.'

'You are. You are annoyed because you didn't notice the difference,' Wendy went on.

'That's nonsense. I knew there was something wrong with those chips. I was just too polite to say.'

Wendy laughed. 'You couldn't tell the difference between White and Wong,' she said and slapped her thigh.

Irene glared over at Wendy. 'I need to go and walk Rocky,' she said.

'Do you want to take these turkey bones with you?... I can wrap them up.'

'Rocky doesn't eat poultry bones,' Irene said. 'They give him the runs.'

Irene got up from the table.

'Well, see yourself out,' Wendy called after her, popping a chip in her mouth.

Theodore wandered back up the hill, past his own house and noticed Belle, sitting on the back wall of Zeynep and Ahmet's house. The two cats sat together while the Turkish couple watched television. Zeynep was sitting with her hands on top of her belly, fingers interlocked. In the corner of the room Theodore noted a leather holdall.

The holdall had been packed and repacked several times in the last days. It contained Zeynep's overnight essentials for when she was taken to hospital. The due date was looming, and the women in her family were not ones for being late.

'I cannot believe that you were having sex with that woman,' Zeynep said. 'When I am expecting your baby…'

Ahmet held his hands out before him. 'OK, OK,' he said. 'I was with her. Is it so hard to understand? We haven't had sex for months.'

'It was uncomfortable for me,' Zeynep said. 'It's not my fault.'

'Yes, I understand. But I have needs.'

'You have needs! You are not supposed to go sleeping around when your wife is pregnant with your baby. You disgust me. I wish you would just leave. I would be better off without you.'

'But I pay the rent. I pay the bills. You need me. The baby needs me.'

'You should have thought about that before you slept with that woman.'

'She means nothing to me. It was just a mistake,' Ahmet said. 'It is over. Can you forgive me?'

'I'm not sure if I can. Or want to.'

'I will make up for it... I will. I will be the perfect father.'

'Do you realize how unhappy I have been,' Zeynep said, beginning to cry. 'Ever since Bal went missing, everything has been just terrible.'

'I promise I will change,' Ahmet said. 'I can make things better.'

Zeynep glared at him.

'I hate you,' she told Ahmet. 'I wish I had never married you.'

'Zeynep. Please.'

A tear slid down her cheek. 'Bal is dead and I might as well be.'

'She might return yet,' Ahmet said. 'Do not give up hope.'

'No,' Zeynep said. 'She is dead; I know it.'

Yellow Fat Disease

Theodore spent the next day catching up on some sleep. He did not wake till he heard Craig unlocking his front door. Time for some tuna, he thought, getting to his feet and stretching.

The tuna dinners had become part of his daily routine. After he had wolfed down his saucer of tuna, he entered the house.

Satisfied that Craig was in the toilet, he hurried upstairs. He had completed his search of Craig's house but had failed to find any incriminating evidence. In the attic he noted that the telescope was still pointing at Diane's bedroom window. The blue curtains were pulled shut even though it was still daylight.

From downstairs, he heard three sharp raps on the front door. He flattened back his ears. In all the weeks of visiting Craig's house, Theodore had never known him have a visitor.

He heard the toilet flush. He jumped down from the back of the chair and raced down the stairs. As he reached the final flight, he saw Craig enter the hallway and approach the front door. Theodore stopped in his tracks halfway down the final flight. If Craig turned round now, he would see Theodore.

Craig inched the front door open.

Emily was on the other side, the remote control for the tracking device pointing at his chest. 'Where is he?' she demanded.

Theodore's tracker was beeping and flashing.

Craig was speechless.

'I know he's in here.'

'Nobody is here except me,' Craig said, staring at the little black box his neighbour was holding. 'I don't know what you're talking about.'

'My cat,' Emily said. 'You've got him in here.'

'I haven't,' Craig began.

'I can see him,' Emily cried. 'He's right behind you.'

Craig turned round to see Theodore on the stairs, his front paws on a lower step to his rear ones.

'I didn't know he was in here,' Craig stuttered. 'I was in the bathroom. I must have left the backdoor open and he wandered in... I just gave him a little bit of tuna.'

'Tuna!' Emily screamed. 'He doesn't eat tuna... 'It gives cats Yellow Fat Disease!'

Emily pushed past Craig and grabbed Theodore up from the stairs. On her way out, she said, 'If you want a cat, go buy your own... Just keep away from mine.'

Once back home, she petted Theodore while Jonathan made two mugs of tea. Her heart was still pounding.

'I'm not going to let him out again,' Emily said. 'He's going to be kept inside from now on.'

Theodore dug his claws into Emily's thighs in protest.

'You can't do that to Theodore,' Jonathan said. 'He loves it outside. He's always in that back alley.'

Emily inspected the tracking device that was fastened to his collar, glad that it had done its job.

'I know what you mean,' she said. 'It would be mean to keep him locked inside all day. I just hope that that guy next door has learned that it's not all right to feed someone else's cat and let it in your house.'

Theodore jumped down from Emily's lap and padded through to the kitchen, before she could change her mind.

Before jumping up onto the back wall, he sharpened his claws on the trunk of the clematis. He worked the bark for some minutes, the shreds joining the growing pile at the foot of the plant.

Mikey's Special Sausage

The smoke from a dozen barbeques fused in the warm evening air. From the backyards came the smell of chicken wings, steaks, burgers, kebabs and sausages cooking over charcoal. The men stood by the makeshift grills, closely monitoring the cooking operation. Cans or little bottles of cold lager within easy reach.

Michael and Philip also had a barbecue in their backyard that evening, and Theodore knew that their sausages were of a superior quality. Michael had bought a selection from a speciality butcher's he had come across at the food fair in Parliament Street that afternoon. He'd opted for ostrich, venison with goose fat, wild boar, and rabbit with jalapeno.

He was wearing a spotless blue and white striped apron over his clothes. He'd had his hair cut that day. Prematurely balding, he now had his hair clipped to within a millimetre of his head at least once a week. He had taken the precaution of smearing sun cream over his stubbly head before lighting the barbeque, but he could still feel his skin turning pink from the sun and heat from the charcoal.

In his hand he held a pair of stainless steel tongs. He turned the spitting sausages and took a sip from his bottle of Belgian beer, a wedge of lime lodged in the neck.

'I think this picture is going to be my breakthrough piece,' he told Philip.

'It's just a drawing of the back alley,' Philip said, taking a swig of beer. He had already downed two bottles while Michael was still on his first.

'Well, you don't look closely enough,' Michael told him, turning a little pinker. 'It's all in the detail.'

'I think your problem is that you can't draw people… People don't want empty streets and alleys. They need to be populated. They need to have human interest.'

'I *can* draw people!' Michael almost shouted.

'I sat for you that time,' Philip said, 'and it looked nothing like me.'

'You kept fidgeting,' Michael said, his cheeks burning. 'You wouldn't keep still… How am I expected to draw someone when they're moving about all the time?'

Deciding to change the subject, Philip said, 'How do you know which sausage is which?'

'I put them in alphabetical order,' Michael said. 'The ostrich on the left. The wild boar on the right…'

'Oh,' Philip said.

Theodore was sitting in the overgrown ivy on top of Michael's wall. He had formed a nest within the plant, so that he was hidden from view. Below him was the barbeque. He eyed the four sausages, neatly lined up.

'I'm going to have the ostrich and the wild boar,' Michael told Philip.

'Looks like I'm having the rabbit and the venison,' Philip said.

'Are you complaining?'

'Of course not… I was just saying.'

'Well, can you keep an eye on them while I go in and butter some baps? They'll be done in a couple of minutes… Just make sure you don't burn them.'

'No problem,' Philip said, taking Michael's place in front of the barbeque.

As soon as Michael was in the kitchen, Philip took from the pocket of his jeans a packet of cigarettes and lit one. He fiddled with the spitting sausages and then went to the corner of the yard, so that he could not be seen from the kitchen window. He was wearing a pair of bright yellow trainers and on his wrist he wore a gold watch which glistened in the sun.

Theodore watched as Philip puffed on his cigarette and swigged from his bottle of beer, gazing up at the cloudless sky. Now was the time to strike.

He got to his paws, jumped silently down into the yard and a second later was standing in front of the barbeque. He singled out the wild boar.

He looked back across the yard. Philip was still smoking, his back to him.

Theodore raised himself up onto his hind legs and, ignoring the fierce heat from the charcoal, dabbed at the end sausage so that it dropped onto the ground. It was still spitting fat as he bit into it. The sausage between his jaws, Theodore jumped back up onto the wall and down the other side. He dropped the sausage to the ground.

It was too hot to eat, so he pawed it across the yard. The old couple who lived in the house next to Michael's were nowhere to be seen, so Theodore decided to let it cool before transporting it to the safety of his own yard. From the other side of the wall, he heard Michael say, 'What's happened to my wild boar?'

'I don't know,' Philip said. 'I really don't know. I was standing over there, and when I looked round there were only three.'

'You've eaten it, haven't you?'

'I haven't. It's just disappeared.'

'Just disappeared? Do you think I'm stupid? Sausages don't just disappear. I told you that I was going to have the wild boar. It was mine.'

'But I didn't touch your sausage,' Philip protested. 'Look Mikey... Someone must have sneaked in and taken it when I wasn't looking.'

'And don't call me Mikey,' Michael said. 'You know I don't like it.'

'Sorry, I forgot,' Philip said. 'But I really didn't take it, Michael. Somebody must have sneaked in and stolen it.'

Theodore heard footsteps approach the back gate, and then the scraping of wood on concrete as the gate was pulled open.

'There's no one out here,' Philip said, scraping the gate closed.

'What a surprise,' Theodore heard Michael mutter.

While the two men were arguing over the missing sausage, Theodore took a bite from the end and began to chew. He had never eaten wild boar before. He wondered momentarily over the ethics of eating animals much larger than himself. Well, he hadn't killed it, he thought, swallowing a piece of sausage.

Next door he heard Michael say loudly: 'It comes down to trust.'

'I really didn't take your sausage, Mikey.'

'Don't call me that!'

Ten minutes later Theodore carried what remained of the sausage through the cat flap. Jonathan was sitting at the dining room table, a newspaper laid out in front of him.

Theodore jumped up and dropped the remaining piece of sausage onto the newspaper.

'A present? For me?' Jonathan said smiling. 'That's very kind of you,' he said, patting Theodore on the head.

Theodore pawed the sausage, so that it rolled towards Jonathan. He had decided that wild boar wasn't for him. He should have gone for the ostrich…

'But it looks like you've singed your fur,' Jonathan said. 'And you've got a pink nose.'

When Emily came downstairs five minutes later, Theodore was still sitting on the table in front of Jonathan.

'Are you two friends now?' she asked.

'Yes, I think we are,' Jonathan said, rubbing Theodore's ears. 'Look he brought me a present.'

He lifted up the grubby sausage to show Emily.

'He brought you a sausage?'

'Yes, he brought it in and dropped it on the paper. He must have raided someone's barbeque. And look: he's singed his fur and burnt his nose.'

Emily picked Theodore up and examined him.

'It does look a bit sore.'

'He's a very brave cat,' Jonathan said.

'Well, I think he likes you now.'

Emily hugged Theodore to her. 'It took a little bit of time for him to get used to you,' she said, 'but he likes you now.'

'Well, I'm glad I've passed the Theodore Test,' Jonathan said.

He picked up the sausage and carried it out to the backyard.

Smoke from barbeques still hung heavy in the air. He checked that Theodore was not watching as he put the sausage in the outside bin. From down the hill he heard two men arguing.

A lovers' quarrel, he thought, as he gently replaced the bin lid.

Wendy Makes a Confession

As summer progressed there was little development in the murder case, either by the police or Theodore. While weeks earlier, it was all that the locals had talked about, it had now evaporated from idle tongues like spring puddles dried out by the summer sun.

While the case file was kept open and any new leads followed up by the police, it seemed more and more unlikely that they would ever catch the Clementhorpe Killer.

It was left to Theodore to carry on the investigation on his own.

He was sitting on the back wall of Wendy Morris's house, eavesdropping as Wendy chatted to her friend Irene.

'Have another biscuit,' Wendy said, gesturing to the plate in the middle of the oval table.

'Don't mind if I do,' Irene said, taking a Viscount. 'I do like a Viscount,' she said, pronouncing the 's'.

'There was a thing on the radio this morning about a dead pigeon,' Irene said, her mouth full of biscuit. 'They went and found a dead pigeon down a chimney somewhere down south. Well, the pigeon had a message strapped to its leg in a little canister or something. But the message was in code so they don't know what it said... They reckon it had been there since the war.'

'Let's hope the message wasn't important,' Wendy said.

Irene took a magazine from a pile on the side board. The title read Gruesome Scenes.

'I don't know how you can read these,' she said, flicking through the magazine.

'I used to read them when I couldn't sleep,' Wendy said. 'But I don't have the stomach for them anymore. I'm going to take them down the charity shop on Bishopthorpe Road... Been having a clear out.'

'The Deep Fat Fryer,' Irene read, her face in the magazine.

'Oh, that's a good one. He was the one that smothered his wife in her sleep,' Wendy said.

'Smothered his wife, did he?' Irene said.

Bill chopped up her body into small parts and started to feed them to his dog. However, the dog turned up its nose at the chunks of raw human flesh, having previously only ever eaten processed dog food. The dismembered body parts were left rotting in the yard. Realizing that the fleshy morsels might begin to attract unwanted attention and flies, he took out his deep fryer and fried them up in beer batter.

While they were cooking the dog began to take an interest, drooling onto the kitchen linoleum. The husband put two pieces of deep fried arm in the dog's bowl, and within five minutes the bowl had been licked clean.

For the next week the dog devoured his former mistress, though it never made the connection.

What the dog wouldn't eat, Bill put beneath the floor boards. However, he was not a carpenter by trade, and when the police came round, at the request of his wife's sister, a bouncy floorboard gave him away.

'Sounds absolutely gruesome,' Irene said, her face still stuck in the magazine. 'Can I borrow it?'

'Of course,' Wendy said, picking out another magazine. 'But this one here's a good one.'

Irene took the proffered magazine from Wendy.

'Bonfire Jack,' she read.

The local girls never took to Jack. 'There was something odd about him, they would all later say,' Irene read aloud.

So Jack imported a wife from Thailand. However, she overdid his steak one day ('Do you not understand what medium rare means?') and so he strangled her, doused her with petrol and put her on the bonfire at the bottom of his garden.

Jack soon became tired of being by himself, having now experienced the love of a woman. So he ordered another Thai wife. His neighbours never even noticed the difference.

This one fared better. She lasted a few months. But then one day she scorched a hole in one of Jack's shirts, having being distracted by the Australian soap opera she had started to watch in the late afternoons. Jack strangled her and added her to his bonfire that was always smouldering away at the bottom of his garden.

The third wife was untidy and within a week was on the bonfire, with the other two. He considered asking for his money back over that one but thought questions might be asked by the agency.

Jack would have ordered a fourth had a neighbour not complained to the council about the smoke. It was ruining her washing, she'd said. The Environmental Health Officer was confronted by the charred corpses when he paid an unannounced visit one morning while Jack was out at work.

'I'll take that one too,' Irene said.

'The Mexborough Chainsaw Mass Killer,' Wendy said, pushing another magazine onto Irene.

The peaceful South Yorkshire town of Mexborough was infamous for fifteen minutes in the 1980s following a killing spree in the town centre. Archibald Templeton, a diagnosed schizophrenic in his mid-thirties, bought a chainsaw, filled it with petrol and headed into town. He first called in at the post office on Main Street, where he butchered twenty people, mainly pensioners. Once he had finished at the post office, the inside of which could only be described as a blood bath, he headed past Teddy's Amusements, through the pedestrianized centre, where he cut up any person not fast enough to get out of his way. Body parts lay scattered where they fell.

The killing spree was brought to a dramatic end in front of the Boy and Barrel when Archibald took the chainsaw to his own head.

The street where Archie put an end to his sad life is now named Hope Street, and the town's Heritage Society have done their utmost to remove all traces of the bloody slaughter from the history books.

'I was wondering why I'd not heard of that one,' Irene said.

'There's the festive special here,' Wendy said, waving another magazine at Irene.

'The Santa Claus Killer,' Irene read, taking a sharp intake of breath. 'No… I think I'll just take these for now.'

'Suit yourself,' Wendy said.

She took a gulp of tea and looked out of her kitchen window. Her eyes met Theodore's.

'That girl's cat is back,' she said. 'I don't know why it bothers now. There's no pigeons left. That black cat had the last one.'

'It's just curious,' Irene said.

'Well, you know what they say,' Wendy said. 'Curiosity…'

'Yes, I know,' Irene interrupted before Wendy could continue.

'Talking of which – I think you should tell Diane,' Irene said. 'Tell her what happened to Arthur. It might put her mind to rest. For all you know she might be thinking he's going to come back some day.'

'I'm not going to tell her,' Wendy said. 'That cat of hers was a menace.'

'It's not right though, and you know it. If you don't tell her, I will.'

'Don't you go telling her,' Wendy said. 'That would really put the cat among the pigeons.' She laughed unconvincingly.

'It's the right thing to do,' Irene said.

Wendy stopped laughing. 'I'll pop round later,' she said. 'I'll tell her myself what happened. Just you keep your nose out of it.'

'You will?'

'Yes, that's what I said. I'll tell her he was knocked down. Then at least she'll know he's not going to come back.'

Theodore listened, not sure if he believed Wendy.

Later he watched as Irene left through Wendy's back gate to take Rocky for his walk.

Theodore made his way along the back walls, up the hill. Ahead of him several people were coming down the hill, towards him.

Balding men with shaven heads, wearing ill-fitting suits; middle-aged women in bright summer dresses and high heels.

They tottered and weaved across the cobbles. Two men stopped to urinate against a gate.

A woman in high heels and short red dress shoved soggy yellow chips into her mouth from a polystyrene tray, spilling them across the cobbles as she lurched forward. Further up the hill, a man lay on the ground, his mobile held in an outstretched hand.

Through the drunken race-goers Zeynep waddled, calling out her cat's name. She smiled up at the grey cat as she passed.

A group of men with red faces and sunglasses then entered the alley. They carried cans of lager that they'd bought at South Bank Stores to keep them fully inebriated on their way to the city centre.

From down the alley, Theodore heard a gate scrape open, and then Michael appeared togged out in a bright pink top and tight black Lycra shorts. He did a few stretches and then began to jog up the hill towards the descending racegoers.

Some moved aside and Michael dodged between the ones that didn't.

As he passed the group, one called out, 'Wanker!' Another one shouted, 'Poofter!' Then another joined in with 'Fudge pusher!'

The group laughed and jeered, and Michael spat on the ground and continued up the alley at a sprint.

They now approached Theodore.

'Look: a cat,' one of them sneered.

'Here pussy, pussy,' another slurred.

Another lobbed his can of lager at Theodore.

Theodore jumped down from the wall, just avoiding the can but getting splashed by lager spray.

The men laughed as Theodore scrambled into the bottom of a hedge. He licked the sticky liquid from his fur as drunken stragglers marched past. He stayed beneath the hedge until the alleyway emptied of people and his annoyance at humankind subsided.

If people spent more time sitting beneath hedges, Theodore thought, the world would surely be a better place.

Just as he was about to cross the alley and head home, Wendy appeared. She walked up the hill and stopped in front of Diane's back gate. After a few moments hesitation, she rapped on the gate.

'Hullo,' she called out. 'Anyone in?'

Shortly the gate was opened and Wendy disappeared inside Diane's yard.

Theodore jumped back up on top of the wall and hurried up to Diane's. *Was she really going to own up to killing Arthur?*

The two women were standing in the kitchen, facing each other.

'I thought you should know,' Wendy said. 'Your cat is not coming back.'

'I know that,' Diane said.

'You do?'

'Yes.'

Diane reached for her packet of cigarettes.

'He was by the side of Scarcroft Road,' Wendy lied. 'Must have been hit by a car.'

Diane lit a cigarette.

'I buried him there in the allotments. I wasn't sure whose cat it was. And I didn't want to leave him lying there.'

'You buried him?' Diane said, blowing out smoke.

'Yes,' Wendy said. 'That's what I said. In the allotments. I didn't want to leave him by the side of the road.'

'That's strange,' Diane said, frowning.

Wendy backed away from the cloud of smoke.

'I buried him in the allotments,' Wendy said. 'I could hardly bury him in my yard... There's no soil in it. I didn't know he was yours, you see. He didn't have a collar on. Then I heard that you had lost your cat and I put two and two together. So here I am.'

Diane blew more smoke at Wendy.

'And then someone dug him up and buried him in their garden?' she said. 'I don't get it.'

'What do you mean?'

'Some guy said that he'd found Arthur in the allotments. He'd taken him and buried him in his garden.'

'I don't know about that,' Wendy said, backing towards the door. 'I just thought you should know. In case you were wondering what had happened to him. I'd better be going.'

Diane said, 'You said you buried him in the allotments. Then someone tells me they found him in the allotments and buried him in their garden. Someone's lying.'

'I buried him in the allotments,' Wendy said. 'Why would I lie about it?'

'Somebody's lying,' Diane repeated and sucked on her cigarette.

'Well, it's not me,' Wendy said.

She turned and walked out of the back door.

Diane exhaled smoke into the air, her forehead creased into four distinct lines.

The Importance of Mrs Columbo

Theodore returned home to find his food bowls empty, his water stagnant and Emily asleep on the sofa in the front room; the shutters closed to the outside world. On the floor there were several silver trays that had held Chinese food.

Theodore kneaded the softness of her stomach through her damp cotton t-shirt but she did not stir. He jumped down and ate the meagre remains from the tinfoil containers.

Among the debris on the floor, he found a brown envelope and a photocopied sheet of paper. On the sheet of paper was a pink post-it. 'Thought this might be useful,' the note read.

Emily's mother must have been to the library again, thought Theodore.

The article was headed: 'Chinese Restaurant Syndrome'.

Theodore read the first paragraph.

'Chinese restaurant syndrome is a set of symptoms that some people have after eating Chinese food. Reports of serious reactions to Chinese food first appeared in 1968. A food additive called monosodium glutamate (MSG) has been blamed for the condition. However, this has not been proven to be the cause. There have been many studies that have failed to show a connection between MSG and the symptoms some people describe.'

If it's not MSG, thought Theodore, what else could it be?

He read on: 'Symptoms include flushing, sweating, headaches, chest pains, numbness or burning in and around the mouth...'

He glanced over at Emily. Her hair was wet with sweat. Her face was puffy and pink. Her lips were red and bloated.

Then he noticed the LED on the answerphone was flashing. He walked over and pressed the button with a paw to play the message, as he had seen Emily do many times.

'It's your mother,' the message announced. 'I've dropped you off some information from the library…'

'All this Chinese food you've been eating, I think it's making you ill. Remember that you are quite intolerant to some foods. There was that time in Spain when you had chilli prawns… You were on the toilet for hours… Both ends.'

Theodore closed his eyes, hoping that further details were not forthcoming.

'Then the time you tried mussels. You've always reacted violently to bivalves. I'm sure I don't have to remind you of the time you had *fruits de mer* on the Algarve…'

Please don't, thought Theodore.

He let the message play to the end with his eyes and ears closed. Then he padded over to a plastic bag and made a note of the address of the Chinese takeaway printed on the side.

Back in the kitchen, he glanced at this empty food bowls again.

What detective can work on an empty stomach, he wondered?

Sherlock Holmes had Mrs Hudson to take care of his everyday needs. Columbo's investigations were never hindered by Mrs Columbo's over fondness for Chinese food. Hercule Poirot dined out a lot, Theodore presumed.

They didn't have to worry where their next meal was coming from. Their needs were taken care of so that they could concentrate their faculties on the case in hand (or paw in Theodore's case).

He realized that he would have to put his own house in order if he was ever going to catch the Clementhorpe Killer. And the only way to do that was to investigate the Lucky Twin.

His tail held straight up, he made for the cat flap.

The Special Ingredient

The back alley behind the Lucky Twin was overgrown, with neither tarmac nor cobblestones adorning the surface. Two parallel lines of bare compacted earth ran the length of the alley, kept free of weeds by the occasional vehicle.

There was a single garage behind the Chinese takeaway, its twin doors opening on to the alley, with a short section of wall to the side, badly spalled on top.

Apart from the garage, the rear of the Lucky Twin was given over to a garden. The garden contained a blanket of purple poppies. The branches of a cherry tree from a neighbouring yard hung over the boundary wall. The branches provided Theodore with a hideout from which he could observe unnoticed.

He had walked over the Big Dipper, to the spot where he'd almost been run over by Diane. Then he had followed his nose, locating the takeaway within a few minutes.

He gazed down at the colourful garden. He longed to jump down and frolic among the flowers, in the soft loamy soil.

But Tony Wong was squatting down among the flowers, his flip-flopped feet straddling the plants. He wore a plain white shirt and black trousers. In his hand he held a small fork, which he used to turn over the soil. Every now and then he tossed a small weed or other undesirable item into a large bowl by his side.

Theodore watched Tony gardening. It was quite relaxing watching humans at work. He closed his eyes, still aware of the man's movements but passing into a half sleep. He only opened them again, almost an hour later, when Tony stood up, took his bowl and entered the back door of the Lucky Twin, through a screen of red, blue and yellow plastic strips.

For a couple of hours Tony worked in the kitchen while Theodore, his eyes closed, quietly appreciated the food aromas.

Later Tony returned to the back garden, a bowl in his hand. Theodore sniffed the air. He made out chicken and fried rice with just a touch of fragrant spice. He considered for a moment jumping down and making himself known to the Chinese man. He hadn't eaten since breakfast and, after his trek over to the takeaway, he could have eaten the whole bowl of chicken and rice. But he held himself back. He was on the job, he reminded himself.

Tony approached the side door to the garage. He opened the door, just wide enough so that he could slip inside. The door shut softly behind him.

Since Arthur had eaten most of his left ear, Theodore now relied on his right. He could hear Tony's voice, speaking softly in Mandarin. Theodore soon tuned into the new language.

'You eat it all up,' Tony was saying. 'You eat it all up. You like my special chicken with rice? Yes, you do, don't you? You eat it all up now.'

Suddenly the screen over the kitchen door parted and Sue Wong appeared. She was shorter and fatter than her husband.

'Tony!' she shouted. 'Where are you, Tony?'

'I'm in here,' Tony called from inside the garage.

'What are you doing in there?'

Tony walked out of the garage and shut the door behind him. 'I was taking stock,' he explained to his wife.

'We need to start preparing the food for this evening,' Sue said. 'You know how busy we are at the moment. We are struggling to keep up with demand.'

'You don't have to tell me,' Tony said. 'I think we need to employ help.'

'I don't think we can afford that,' Sue said. 'You know very well how much the school fees are at the Mount. We only just managed to scrape together enough for this term's boarding.'

Tony shook his head. 'I knew we should have just had one child.'

'I couldn't help it that we had twins,' Sue said smiling.

'Well, it will all be worth it one day,' Tony said. 'Our daughters will be captains of industry!'

'Yes,' Sue said, 'they won't have to work in a takeaway, preparing crispy duck and fish and chips their whole lives.'

'They won't have to smell of curry sauce and fried rice,' her husband agreed. 'Now we must get on.'

After Sue had returned inside, Tony went back into the garage. A moment later Theodore watched as Tony returned with an empty bowl in his hand and carried it into the kitchen where he placed it with the rest of the washing up in the large metal sink in front of the window.

The kitchen was small and overflowing with the makings of the two hundred items on the Lucky Twin's takeaway menu. There were a half dozen saucepans of different sauces simmering away. Tony could turn around any item on the menu within two minutes of Sue handing over the order. It was all in the preparation.

But the volume leaving the kitchen in recent weeks had reached an unprecedented level. In the four hours between six and ten o'clock, Tony was putting out around three hundred dishes. At ten to ten Sue was shutting the door and any customers still queuing in the street were sent away.

From time to time Sue walked in to inspect how the food preparations were going and remind Tony of how long it was until they opened their door to the street.

'Two hours 'til opening,' she informed Tony at four o'clock.

Theodore closed his eyes and napped briefly.

He opened his eyes some time later when he heard footsteps approaching along the back alley. He was well concealed by the branches of the cherry tree, so was not worried that he would be seen by whoever was approaching. But then the footsteps kept coming closer until they came to a stop less than a yard away.

A man's head had joined Theodore in the canopy of the tree. He didn't notice Theodore. His stare was fixed at Tony, still busy in the kitchen.

The man was in his mid-sixties. His dyed blond hair was scraped back from his face and combed back across his head. The grey scalp of his head was visible in the furrows left by the steel comb that he carried in the top pocket of his jacket. He wore steel rimmed glasses and a dark blue suit. His canary-yellow shirt was open at the neck. Theodore smelled a hint of aftershave underlined by a slightly fishy odour.

They both watched as Tony placed a dozen ducks into oven dishes on the kitchen side. There was a neat row of glass jars on the kitchen windowsill, filled with herbs and spices. They watched as Tony picked out a small jar without a label and took a fair-sized pinch and began to sprinkle it over the ducks.

Sue was observing from the doorway. 'Make sure you don't use too much of that special ingredient,' Sue said.

'We have plenty,' Tony said.

'We mustn't run out of it… Our customers would soon go and find another outlet for their cravings.'

'I am being careful, Sue,' Tony said, screwing the lid back on the jar and returning it to the windowsill.

Sue turned and walked out of the kitchen, glancing at her wristwatch as she went.

Tony busied himself with the tasks of seasoning, salting, boiling, rubbing, drying, roasting and glazing the duck, following an ancient recipe handed down by his father back in Chongqing.

Theodore heard more footsteps approaching along the alley. Then the man by his side stepped away from the wall.

'Why, Frank White!' Irene said. 'Whatever are you doing over there with your head in that tree?'

'Oh, hallo there,' Frank White said, backing away from the wall.

Theodore turned to see Irene, her dog Rocky straining on its lead three yards in front of her.

'Fancy seeing you here,' Irene said.

'I was just having a little walk,' Frank said. 'I must have wandered into that there tree... It needs a good cropping.'

'You need to get your eyes tested Frank,' Irene chided. 'I was just out with Rocky.'

Frank White bent down and patted the German shepherd on the head. The dog licked his hand excitedly. Frank took his handkerchief from his jacket pocket and wiped away the saliva.

'Oh, I'm sorry, Frank,' Irene said. 'He gets a bit excited around men. He doesn't get much male company, you see. A bit like myself.'

Frank smiled. 'Don't worry about it. No harm done.' He refolded his handkerchief and returned it to his jacket pocket.

'I could wash it for you,' Irene offered.

'There really is no need,' Frank said.

'All right, Frank,' Irene said.

There was a moment's awkward silence.

'It was terrible what happened to Peter Morris,' Irene said. 'Who would want to do such a thing?'

'I wasn't that surprised,' Frank said. 'To tell the truth.'

'Oh?'

'Well, he wasn't liked… At the club,' he said. 'He had an opinion on everything… And many of his opinions were not that nice… I wasn't all that surprised when I heard.'

'He went to kick Rocky once,' Irene said, nodding. 'He got into his yard… and he said that he'd stirred up his birds. Went at him, he did… He was going to kick him.'

'Aye, I wasn't all that surprised,' Frank said. 'He would have wound up the wrong person.'

'Aye, he must have said something to someone,' Irene said.

'Aye. He'd have upset someone.'

Then Frank said, 'I'd better be going. The shop…'

'Yes, of course,' Irene said. 'Bye Frank.'

'Bye Irene.'

Frank began to walk along the alley in the direction from which Irene had come.

When he was about twenty yards away, Irene called after him, 'I'll be in later for me chips!'

Frank turned and waved goodbye to Irene. Over her shoulder he noticed a grey smudge on top of the wall, amongst the branches of a cherry tree. He realized that it was a cat. The cat stared back at him. Had it been there a minute ago?

Irene returned Frank's gaze through her own myopic eyes. For a minute she was back in the school classroom, exchanging long, meaningful looks with the boy with the tousled hair. She had always thought he had not noticed her back then. But he evidently remembered her now. She could tell by the way he stared back at her.

Before her daydreaming could progress, Irene was rudely jerked around by Rocky, who had also noticed Theodore on the wall.

'Rocky!' she admonished.

The German shepherd barked excitedly.

Irene yanked the dog's lead and managed to pull him away.

'I don't know what's got into him,' she called after Frank, who was almost at the bottom of the alley.

Frank did not turn round. He marched onwards, towards his fish and chip shop.

Theodore watched as Tony removed the ducks from the oven. He placed them on the kitchen counter and took two forks from a drawer. With practised skill he shredded the meat from the bones and then tossed the duck carcasses in the bin; the meat he placed in a large tray he covered with tinfoil.

Theodore's chin was wet with drool. His stomach hurt with hunger. His instinct was to jump down into the garden and raid the kitchen, and then make his escape. But Theodore restrained himself. He watched as Tony covered the dish with tinfoil and placed it back in the oven to keep warm. Tony glanced at the clock on the kitchen wall.

At six o'clock Sue called out, 'Are you ready? I'm going to open the door.'

'I'm ready,' Tony shouted back.

Tony Wong worked without a break. From the front of the shop Sue Wong took the orders, relentlessly slapping order chits on the counter that separated the front of the shop from the kitchen. Seeing Tony busy in the kitchen, Theodore jumped down into the garden.

He examined the soil. There was a shallow depression where he had landed. He had not been the first cat to jump into this garden, he realized.

He spotted old paw prints in the soil extending from the landing site and into the wilderness of poppies that towered above him.

He followed a cat trail through the poppies. In a small clearing, the soil had been disturbed in several discrete patches. He sniffed at the little mounds; he knew that none of the piles were fresh.

In front of him there was the kitchen window. To his side there was the garage. The soil was soft and damp beneath his paws. He looked at the patches of disturbed soil. Like Pavlov's dog, he was a prisoner to suggestion.

He dug a small hole and squatted down. He was in the middle of his bowel movement when the back door swung open.

'Not again,' Tony said, a kitchen knife held in one hand.

Theodore cut it short.

'You do not mess in my garden,' Tony cried, coming towards Theodore, the knife raised.

Theodore turned tail and did not look back until he was back on top of the wall, shielded by the branches of the cherry tree.

'And do not come back,' Tony shouted after him, waving the knife.

Sue appeared in the doorway. 'What is going on?' she asked. 'We have customers waiting for their orders…'

Tony turned to her. 'A cat,' he said. 'He was in the garden. He was messing in the garden.'

'We have customers waiting for their meals and you are playing with cats in the garden.' Sue shook her head, arms folded, then turned and walked back to her position behind the counter.

Tony returned to the kitchen, where he was kept busy preparing meals until ten o'clock, then spent another hour cleaning the kitchen. Sue joined him and helped scrub the ovens and the hobs, while Tony scrubbed pans in the sink. They then counted up the takings.

'Not a bad evening,' Tony said, pushing crumpled notes into a brown A4 envelope.

'We should soon have enough for next term's school ski trip,' Sue said with a sigh.

'It is lucky that they let us pay in instalments. I don't know how other parents manage.'

'One day it will all be worth it,' Sue said.

They turned off the downstairs lights and moments later lights were turned on and curtains drawn upstairs. Theodore waited until the upstairs lights had been turned off before he jumped down into the garden again and finished the business he'd started earlier.

The bedroom window was open to the night-time air. From inside he could hear Sue and Tony talking quietly.

Later, when he heard Tony snoring, he approached the side door to the garage. He pressed his good ear to the timber door.

He couldn't hear anything from inside. He miaowed softly.

A raspy miaow echoed back from behind the wooden door.

He miaowed again. Again the miaow was returned.

There were no windows to the garage. He paced up and down in front of the door. He noticed a spade leant against the garage wall. What good is a spade to me? he thought glancing at his paws.

He retreated to the back wall and jumped up onto the top. Where the wall abutted the garage, he managed to jump up onto its sloping slate-tiled roof. He walked across the slates until he reached the ridge. He glanced over to the two upstairs windows of the Lucky Twin. He could still make out Tony's snores.

He walked along the ridge and spotted a rectangular panel of glass, silver in the moonlight, set into the grey slate roof. He peered through the roof light.

A large chest freezer stood against the back wall. Numerous cardboard boxes were stacked in the remaining space.

Theodore realized that the boxes were not tight up against the wall. There was a gap about two feet wide between the boxes and the wall, forming a run the length of the garage. At one end of the run two bowls were placed, one with water and one with food, next to a cushion. At the other end of the run was a tray containing what appeared to be uncooked rice, dotted with small turds. Pacing between the bowls and the litter tray was a cream coloured cat.

Theodore dabbed a paw on the glass.

From below a tabby face peered up at him. Her blue eyes penetrated the darkness. There was no doubt that it was Bal, Belle's missing sister.

But Bal was almost twice the size of Belle. Her diet of fried rice, chicken and whatever else Tony had been feeding her along with her confinement in the garage had led to this state of obesity. Bal stared up at Theodore, her eyes pleading to be released from her makeshift prison.

Theodore understood at once what must have happened. Tony had discovered Bal fouling his precious garden. Unable to harm the cat, he had locked her in the garage and kept her prisoner.

Theodore miaowed through the glass that he would get her out.

But how am I to spring Bal from her cell? he wondered.

His question was answered by a whistling from the alley.

The Naked Chippie

Theodore descended to the eaves of the garage and crouched above the gutter. He watched as Frank White's head appeared over the back wall.

Frank was now dressed in a black polo neck jumper. His dyed blond hair was waxed back from his face. He stood behind the wall for a minute, surveying the back of the Lucky Twin.

Then he placed his forearms on the top of the wall and heaved himself up and over to the other side.

'Oh, my knees,' he cried, landing in the garden.

He made for the side of the garage, just below the spot where Theodore was crouching.

What was Frank up to? Theodore wondered.

He watched as Frank approached the kitchen window. The top had been left ajar, no doubt to air the kitchen overnight. Frank took from his pocket a piece of string. Theodore noted that it had already been tied into a noose at one end.

Frank held open the window with one hand and with the other hand fed through the noose, lowering it until it was level with the window fastener. He was a short while attempting to hook the loop of the noose over the edge of the fastener but with a quietly exclaimed 'Yes!' he succeeded. He jerked on the string and the fastener lifted. Frank swung open the kitchen window.

On the inside of the window ledge stood the row of jars. Frank grabbed one of the jars and unscrewed the lid. 'Now,' he said, 'we shall see what this special ingredient is all about'.

He stuck his forefinger into his mouth, sucked on it a second, then thrust the finger into the jar before putting it back into his mouth. He smacked his lips. 'As I thought: monosodium glutamate and...?'

He thrust his finger in again. 'Something else... Something else, indeed.'

He shook more of the powder into his mouth straight from the jar. 'It really is quite tasty... Reminds me of... Burma.'

He smacked his lips.

'Aye, Burma!' he said, a flashback to his days in the merchant navy.

Theodore watched as Frank held the jar above his head, then tipped the entire contents into his mouth.

His eyes grew wide and sweat began to bead on his wrinkled forehead. 'It's damned good... It is a pity that it's all gone!'

He held the empty jar in front of his face. 'What a pity!' he cried. 'It's all gone!' He opened his mouth wide and laughed.

The light in the upstairs bedroom flicked on and the curtain turned poppy red. There were hurried steps on the stairs. Then the kitchen light was turned on, bathing the garden in white light.

Theodore saw Tony Wong in black silk pyjamas rush into the kitchen. He grabbed a kitchen knife and made for the kitchen door.

Frank abruptly stopped laughing. He dropped the jar. It shattered on the concrete paving slab at his feet.

As Tony unlocked the door, Frank turned and ran to the back wall.

The kitchen door swung open.

Theodore blinked. It was time for action.

As Tony rushed outside, knife in hand, Theodore jumped down from the garage roof and into the poppy garden. Tony saw the cat and swung round, swiping at him with the knife. But Theodore jumped out of his way, kicking up soil behind him. Tony swiped again with the blade but once more Theodore jumped out of his reach, kicking up dirt behind him.

Theodore saw Frank scrambling up and over the back wall to safety, then made his own escape towards the branches of the cherry tree in the opposite corner of the yard. From the top of the wall he turned and saw Sue standing in red silk pyjamas in the doorway.

'What's going on out here, Tony?'

Tony turned to his wife. 'We have been raided,' he said.

'Excuse me?'

'An old man and a big fluffy cat. They raided us... The special ingredient is all gone.'

He pointed at the broken glass on the floor. 'It is all gone.'

He pushed his fingers through his hair.

'But what are we to do?' Sue said. 'Without the special ingredient our business will be ruined... Our competitive edge is gone... The twins will have to go to a state school. They will no longer be Mount Girls...'

'I'm sure it won't come to that,' Tony said.

'We are ruined,' Sue said.

'I will make more,' Tony said. 'We still have the poppies. We will have to be careful for a while.'

'We'll get through this, won't we Tony?'

'Yes, Sue. Of course... It is just a set back to our operation. Let us go back to bed and we shall clear this mess up in the morning... Then I will go to B&Q and buy more security. I will install CCTV...'

'We must make sure that this cannot happen again.'

'I will lock up and then we will go back to bed. There is nothing more we can do tonight.'

Theodore watched from behind the tree's foliage, as Tony locked the back door, closed the kitchen window, turned off the lights and followed Sue back up to bed. The garden was in darkness again. He glanced over at the garage in which Bal was imprisoned.

Further up the alley he saw Frank doing squat thrusts.

Theodore jumped down and approached Frank.

'I guess I should be thanking you,' Frank panted. 'A lucky escape that.'

Theodore rubbed himself against the bottom of Frank's trousers.

'You got me out of a tight spot back there,' he went on. 'My name's Frank White. You can call me Frank.'

Frank smiled, exposing his capped front teeth. They shone white in the moonlight.

'I feel like walking,' he said. 'I am full of beans. I haven't felt this good for years!'

Frank walked to the top of the alley and did a star jump. Theodore followed.

Frank marched with long strides up Queen Victoria Street, past the Knavesmire pub on the corner, and onto Knavesmire Road, flanked by grassland on both sides. Theodore had to trot every now and again to keep up with the fish and chip shop proprietor.

They wandered out onto the Knavesmire, ominously flat and vast in the moonlight. Several cars were scattered where they had been parked the afternoon before; their owners too drunk to drive.

Frank broke into a gallop. 'I feel like running!' he shouted. 'Come on, Cat!'

Although Theodore didn't like being addressed as 'Cat', he trotted after Frank.

Frank hurdled the plastic railings that demarcated the racecourse and began to sprint along the well-tended turf. 'I am a racing horse!' he shouted. 'I am a wild stallion!'

As he ran he pulled his polo neck over his head and flung it behind him. His steel framed spectacles fell by the wayside. Then off came his white vest, followed by his shoes, his socks, his chinos and finally his underpants, which Theodore dodged as he raced after the now naked Frank.

His lean body was muscled from his high protein, high carbohydrate diet of fish and chips, his forty press-ups a day, forty sit-ups, and then forty squeezes on his bullworker.

But what surprised Theodore was the artwork that festooned Frank's body. Across his chest, his back, his torso, were dozens of pictures of foreign climes, exotic beauties, and strange beasts: mementos of his life in the merchant navy. In each foreign port, his body had been inked; the tattoos were stamps on the passport that was his body.

Frank suddenly stopped, turned and faced Theodore. His chest hair was silver in the moonlight. The hair on his head remained golden, wet with sweat, plastered back across his head.

He raised a fist in the air, his legs apart. 'I will not stand for it any longer,' he shouted.

His body dripping with sweat; his eyes insanely wide, he shouted into the night, 'I will put an end to their dodgy dealings!'

And with this proclamation, Frank White lay down on the soft turf. His mouth open an inch, his capped upper teeth sticking out, he began to snore.

There Can Be Only One Willow

The night grew cold.

Theodore tried to wake Frank White, who was laid out star-shaped on the flat turf of the race track. He scratched at his chest and dabbed at his face with the pads of his paws, but Frank was out cold, his blood cooling by the minute. Fearing the old man might not make it through the night, Theodore settled on his chest, allowing his body heat to flow into Frank's. He fell asleep to the patter of Frank's heart.

As dawn broke over York and the racecourse, Theodore stirred. Frank was trembling beneath him.

In the distance a sortie of seagulls strutted across the turf.

Theodore located Frank's glasses and carried them back along the racetrack to where Frank lay. He dabbed at his face with the pads of his paws and Frank stirred.

His eyes, bloodshot and red rimmed, flashed open.

'The racecourse! How did I get here? Where are my clothes? My glasses?'

He noticed the fluffy grey cat standing by his side, his glasses at its paws. He sat up and put on his glasses.

He grabbed his black polo neck and pulled it over his head. He glanced about, wondering where the rest of his clothes were, and why he was in the middle of the racecourse. He slapped his forehead with the palm of his hand.

'I remember now!' he said. 'The special ingredient... We must make sure those Wongs cannot continue destroying the minds of the good people of York. We must put a stop to their opiate foolery. Yes, we must finish what we have started. We must destroy the poppy garden! What do you think, Cat?'

Theodore rubbed himself against Frank's side and purred in agreement. Frank was evidently still affected by his overdose of the opiate-laced secret ingredient.

'Good. Now where are my underpants. We must strike while the iron is hot!'

Theodore raised his tail aloft and led Frank to his underpants.

His clothes retrieved and fully dressed, Frank made his way back across the racecourse, Theodore at his side.

It had just turned six o'clock; the bells of York Minster told them so. The first dog walkers had yet to venture out. Apart from Fred's Bakery that they passed on the corner of Albemarle Road, there were no signs of life.

Frank paused as he passed his fish and chip shop. He looked up at the red and blue sign over the shop window:

THE BATTER'D SEA CODS' HOME
THE PLAICE FOR QUALITY FISH & CHIPS
PROPRIETOR – MR F. WHITE
("THE COD FATHER")

When he thought of the name back in the nineties, he had been pleased with the puns. But now the paint had flaked from the sign and the colours faded.

He shook his head and then clapped his hands together.

'I reckon we should have enough time to deal with the Wongs and be back in time to fry up some fish for breakfast,' Frank said. 'What do you say, Cat?'

Theodore rubbed himself against Frank's calves and miaowed his approval. They continued down Queen Victoria Street.

As they approached the Lucky Twin, Frank took from his trouser pocket his stainless steel comb and combed back his hair. He brushed grass from his chinos with the backs of his hands. He plucked some grass from his polo neck jumper and then hitched up his imitation snake skin belt.

From the shelter of the cherry tree they surveyed the rear of the property. The curtains were still closed. No lights were on. The Wongs were still in bed.

From the street they heard the milkman whistle as he delivered pints to those customers who still preferred their milk in glass bottles. Frank glanced at his watch and waited for the second hand to complete a minute.

'Time to act!' he cried, and launched himself on top of the wall and down the other side in one swift movement.

Theodore followed shortly after, landing in the soft earth of the poppy garden seconds after Frank.

Then they went to work. Theodore employed his back legs to unearth the plants, while Frank yanked them from the ground and launched them high into the air. Within ten minutes all the plants had been uprooted and scattered across the garden. Frank stamped on them as they lay in the dirt.

'I think our work here is done, Cat,' Frank declared.

Theodore miaowed no.

'What is it, Cat?'

Theodore approached the side door to the garage. He miaowed again.

His miaow was echoed from inside.

'There's a cat in there, is there?' Frank said, approaching the door. 'We must get it out!'

He tried the door but it was locked.

He looked around and noticed the spade against the garage wall. He slid it into the gap between the door and the wall, above the lock, and pushed down hard. The door swung open with a loud creak and splintering of wood. He replaced the spade against the wall and entered the garage.

It took a few moments to focus in the dim light. He scanned the boxes of ingredients piled precariously high, the chest freezer against the back wall, and the industrial-sized bags of rice.

Bal miaowed once more, and Frank's eyes were drawn to the wall of boxes.

'So that's where you are,' he said, approaching the boxes.

He began to move a tower of boxes, stacking them one by one onto the top of the chest freezer. Theodore kept watch at the door.

'There we go!' Frank said. 'What a fat cat!'

Bal was almost identical to Belle, though she had indeed put on weight during her weeks of captivity. Her fur was matted.

She purred as Theodore examined her. She would be all right, he thought.

Theodore led her out of the garage, and Frank opened the gate and let them out into the alley.

'Well, it was good working with you,' Frank said. 'You get yourselves home now, Cats.'

Then they parted their ways. Frank strolled away towards Queen Victoria Street and his fish and chip shop, and the two cats towards their homes in Clementhorpe.

Shortly after eight o'clock, Tony and Sue Wong rose from bed, dressed and opened the curtains. They looked out at their garden.

'Our garden!' Tony cried. 'It has been destroyed.'

'Who would do such a thing!' exclaimed Sue.

'Little Rosie and Lily will have to go to Millthorpe School now,' said Tony, shaking his head.

'We are in the wrong business,' Sue said. 'We should have set up a late night disco like Tommy Fong did. The Willow has made him millions over the years… He doesn't even cook food anymore. He just hands out prawn crackers… The students are so drunk they don't care.'

'I don't like students,' said Tony.

'Don't be silly,' Sue said. 'Our daughters will be students when they go to university. Will you not like them then?'

'No,' Tony said. 'That is different. They are our little girls.'

'Maybe Tommy Fong didn't like students,' Sue said. 'But he was happy to take their money and smile. Now he is a very rich man and they say he will retire to Filey.'

'Maybe you should have married Tommy Fong,' Tony said.

'Stop being silly,' Sue said. 'I married you. We must persevere with the Lucky Twin.'

'Yes,' Tony agreed. 'We must persevere with the Lucky Twin.

'We must make sure Rosie and Lily remain Mount Girls,' Sue went on.

'I will buy more poppy seeds when I go to B&Q this morning... And I will make sure no old men or big fluffy cats can penetrate our garden again.'

'We will get through this,' Sue said determinedly. 'One day it will all be worth it.'

'Yes,' Tony said. 'We will get through this. Our daughters will benefit from the education that we didn't have…'

Cat Confessional

Theodore led Bal along the back alleys to Clementhorpe.

The Birman cat lagged behind and had to stop frequently to rest. But as they neared Avondale Terrace, she recognized smells from before her incarceration and, with tail held aloft, trotted across the blue cobbles towards her gate. She paused in front of the gate and miaowed, a long raspy miaow.

From inside, another cat miaowed back. Belle shortly jumped up onto the back wall and then down into the alley. She rubbed against her sister, purring loudly. She licked Bal's fur and Theodore joined in. By the time they had finished, Bal's fur was slicked back but matted clumps still stood proud.

Then Theodore began a caterwauling and the two Birmans joined in.

Zeynep snapped open her curtains. Then she hurried downstairs.

'Bal?' she cried as she came out into the yard. 'Is that you, Bal?' She swung open the back gate and saw the three cats.

She collected Bal in her arms and hugged her. 'Bal,' she cried. 'You've come back!'

She laughed. But then her laughter turned to tears and she broke down. 'Oh Bal,' she spluttered, carrying the cat inside. 'I've done something terrible.'

Theodore took up position on the back wall and was soon joined by Belle. They watched as Zeynep sat down at her kitchen table, holding Bal beneath her chin, the cat resting on top of her bulge.

'I thought that pigeon man had done something to you,' Zeynep said.

Then she told Bal what she had done.

147

Ahmet had been out at work, doing his evening shift, so Zeynep had gone out to look for Bal.

She had walked down the alley and near the bottom she heard a murmuring from a yard. She realized it must be the pigeon man talking to his birds. She remembered what Ahmet had said about people who kept birds not liking cats.

She approached the back gate. Standing in the glare cast by the security light, she listened to the man mumbling away to his birds from behind the wall.

She would ask him if he'd seen her cat. She would ask him if he could check his shed. She would find out if he had done something to Bal.

She rapped on the gate. Peter Morris went quiet.

She rapped again, a little louder.

Then she heard soft-slippered footsteps approach the gate.

'Hullo?' he said from the other side.

'Hello,' Zeynep said. 'I live up the street.'

'How can I help?' Peter said.

'Can I speak to you for a moment?'

A moment passed and then the gate opened.

Peter Morris stood in the gateway. In his hands he held a plump pigeon.

'Yes?' he said. 'What is it?'

'My cat has gone missing,' Zeynep began, 'and I was wondering...'

Peter sucked in the cool night air between his teeth.

'I thought she may be in your shed,' Zeynep went on. 'She might have got locked in.'

'Look,' Peter said, stepping aside, so that Zeynep could see past him and into the outbuilding, 'there's no cat in there. See for yourself.'

Zeynep looked into the outbuilding. There was no cat.

'Just because I keep pigeons,' Peter muttered, 'doesn't mean I've done something to your bloody cat.'

'I didn't say you did.'

Peter shook his head from side to side.

'I know you,' he said. 'You're married to that taxi driver fellow, aren't you? I've seen him coming out of No.24. He's been having it off with that Lancashire hotpot. That's what he's been up to…'

'Excuse me?' Zeynep said.

'You heard… He's been having sex with that tart from No.24. Don't you understand English?'

'Tart?'

'Diane,' Peter said. 'Her from the wrong side of the Pennines. He's been having it off with her.'

Zeynep was stunned into silence for a moment, by Peter Morris's rudeness and also the fact that her husband was having sex with one of her neighbours when she was carrying his child.

Then she said slowly, 'What's it got to do with you?'

'What's it got to do with me?' Peter said excitedly. 'I live here, that's what.'

'I live here too. Here is my home.'

'You don't understand. I live here. I was born here. You lot should go and clear off back where you came from.'

'You lot?' Zeynep's cheeks glowed with anger.

Peter began to close the gate on her. 'Yes, you lot!'

Zeynep pushed back against the gate, sending Peter falling backwards into his outbuilding. The events that followed were a bit of blur in her mind; it happened so quickly.

She remembered the pigeon scrabbling about on the floor of the yard. She remembered the old man's grunts as he lay on the floor of his outbuilding, seed spilling onto him from an upturned sack. He was on his hands and knees, trying to get to his feet, his back to Zeynep.

She spotted the cobblestone holding the door open. She picked it up. Then she hit him on the back of the head with it before he could get to his feet.

Pigeons scattered into the night, their wings beating white against the dark sky.

'He was groaning in pain,' Zeynep gasped into Bal's fur. 'I ran up the alley, I threw the cobblestone over a wall as I passed. I got home. I sat here at the kitchen table… Waiting for Ahmet to come home. I was going to tell him everything. I waited and he didn't come… I was going to tell him what I'd done, but he didn't come home…

'Hours passed and I went up to bed… I couldn't sleep. Then I heard him come in. And I thought he would come up and check on me, but he didn't. He started doing laundry. Then I knew it was true. He had been with her. I decided not to tell him what I'd done…

'But I killed him. That horrible old man. I killed him.

'I didn't know it. Not until I heard later that he was dead.

'Then I knew that I'd killed him.'

Zeynep's face was buried in Bal's fur.

'I did it,' she spluttered. 'I killed him. I killed Peter Morris.'

She looked down to where a pool was growing on the linoleum between her feet. She placed Bal on the table and reached for her mobile.

'Ahmet,' she said into her phone. 'It is time.'

What the Cat Brought In

Theodore listened as Ahmet's taxi started up and the Turkish couple departed for York Hospital. The two Birman cats, Bal and Belle, sat on the dining table and waited. They weren't aware that the peace of their home was about to be shattered by a squalling usurper. Rather you than me, thought Theodore.

He turned tail and jumped down into the back alley. He was pleased with himself. He had managed to reunite Bal with her owner. He had helped to put a temporary stop to the Lucky Twin's operation, and he knew who had killed Peter Morris. Not bad work, he thought, as he padded softly across the cobbles. He now just needed to prove that he hadn't eaten any pigeon.

He jumped up on the back wall of Diane's house. Her bedroom curtains were drawn. She was still in bed. It was Sunday morning after all, and she had no cat to get her out of bed.

In the undergrowth among Arthur's dried turds, he discovered the bones of a pigeon's leg encircled in a hard plastic ring. A string of letters and numbers carved into the ring could prove that the leg had once belonged to a certain pigeon that had gone missing at the start of summer.

Theodore cast his mind back to the morning he had discovered Peter Morris's body in the shed. Arthur had been cleaning himself in the back alley by his back gate. Evidently he had eaten the bird while Theodore had still been asleep. He recalled something his mother had once said to him about the early cat catching the bird.

Theodore took the thin bones encircled in plastic and carried them home. As he entered the kitchen, Emily jumped up from the dining room table.

151

'Theodore,' she cried. 'Where have you been?'

She grabbed him up and hugged him to her. 'I've been up half the night worrying.'

'I told you he'd come back,' Jonathan said, not looking up from the Sunday papers.

Theodore dropped his package of bones onto the Review.

'Ugh!' Jonathan said with a grimace. 'Look what he's brought in…'

'Eh!' Emily said. 'What is it?'

'I think it's part of a dead bird,' Jonathan said, prodding the bones with his forefinger. 'And there's a plastic ring.'

'Not again,' Emily said. 'Just put it in the bin… Outside.'

Theodore looked on as Jonathan carried the newspaper supplement with the pigeon remains outside.

It was definitely time for a nap, he thought, as he heard the bin lid being replaced with a clatter.

The Case Is Altered

Theodore went to sleep on Emily's bed sound in the knowledge that he had solved the case. He knew that Zeynep had killed Peter Morris and Arthur had eaten Ethel. What he would do with the information was another matter.

It was late afternoon when he stirred. Through the open window, he could hear voices. One voice he recognized straightaway as Emily's. The other he soon realized was Michael's.

He heard Michael say, 'Haven't seen you in a while... Not since...'

'No,' Emily said. 'Not since *that* morning.'

Every few seconds Michael took a sharp intake of breath, and Theodore understood that he was running on the spot.

'How's the drawing going?' Emily asked.

'Good,' Michael said. 'I've started on a new series.'

'Oh, yes?'

'Portraiture...'

'How exciting!'

'I'm looking for a new model actually.'

'Oh, yes?' Emily said. 'What happened to the last one?'

She laughed but Michael didn't.

'You have quite an interesting face,' he said, breathing hard. 'Some interesting curves.'

'Well, no one's said that about it before!'

'Perhaps you can sit for me sometime?'

'Like model?'

'Yes, like model,' Michael said. 'Though you'll just have to sit still... No fidgeting!'

'Modelling?' Emily said. 'Why not?'

'That's great.'

'Me a model!' Emily said and laughed. 'When?'

'This evening?' Michael said, 'If you don't have anything else planned.'

'I've got no plans for this evening.'

'Well, I'll see you later then. Say seven? I'd better get on... I want to do two laps round the racecourse before dinner...'

'All right,' Emily said. 'See you at seven.'

Theodore listened as Michael panted off up the back alley and Emily returned inside.

Theodore tried to go back to sleep but something nagged at his mind. When he had gone to sleep he had been confident that the case was solved. Now he wasn't so sure. He began to think over the facts.

Peter Morris, it transpired, hadn't been a particularly nice man. He'd told Zeynep that her husband had been having an affair. He had made a racist remark to her. Zeynep had hit him over the head with a cobblestone. She had fled the scene. She had thrown the cobblestone in Craig's garden as she dashed by.

So far, so good.

Theodore did not doubt for a moment what Zeynep had confessed to Bal. What owner would lie to their cat?

But something did not add up.

He cast his mind back, searching for clues, thinking over the details. He went right back to the beginning, before he'd discovered the body of Peter Morris.

He had entered the back alley, smelling the morning air.

There were the smells of other cats, the fragrance from what flora grew, the human generated waste that lay decomposing in rubbish bins, the faint smell of cocoa hanging in the air...

He knew that the local chocolate factory, Terry's, had closed down some years earlier, and they were starting to build houses on the site. The other chocolate factory, Rowntrees, was located on the northern side of York.

Had the wind blown the smell of cocoa across the city? he wondered.

He remembered the wind had blown the feathers and other debris in Peter Morris's yard mainly towards the wall opposite the gate and not the other way. The wind had been blowing from the south that morning. Theodore realized that it couldn't have been the Rowntrees factory that he had smelled that morning.

The only other explanation was that someone had been up and made cocoa before the sun had risen.

Who drank cocoa?

'Me, I like a mug of cocoa in the morning,' Wendy had told Laura after Peter's funeral.

So Wendy was already awake when he had entered the yard and discovered Peter's body. She hadn't been woken by Emily's scream, as she'd claimed.

He remembered Wendy unlocking her back door and entering her yard. She had on her fur-lined slippers. If someone screamed in your yard, would you stop to put on your slippers? No, Wendy had been awake; awake and waiting.

Theodore got to his paws. If Wendy had already been awake, why did she claim that she'd been woken by Emily's scream?

He then remembered Zeynep's confession. 'He was groaning in pain,' she'd told Bal.

So when Zeynep fled the scene, Peter was still alive, and when Theodore discovered the body, Wendy was already awake.

'He wouldn't have known what hit him,' the police officer had told Wendy.

Theodore remembered the state of Peter Morris's head that morning. He wouldn't have been lying groaning in pain with an injury like that.

Zeynep might have hit him on the head with a cobblestone, but someone else had finished him off with something else.

That someone had to be his wife, Wendy, Theodore concluded. She had whacked him over the back of the head with her rolling pin.

He stirred from the bed, got to his paws and stretched.

The case is definitely altered, he thought.

Wendy Puts Out Her Rubbish

Shortly after six o'clock, Wendy put out her rubbish. She opened her back gate and carried her two black bin bags outside and placed them against the side wall of her house.

Theodore knew from his reconnaissance that he only had a few seconds. As soon as her back was turned he dashed from the corner of the alley and through the open gate.

He was inside the house. He made for the stairs. He paused on the landing.

The front bedroom was painted salmon pink, a double bed with pink duvet. The back bedroom was magnolia with a single bed up against the window. Theodore understood that Peter and Wendy had slept in separate bedrooms, and the back bedroom was where Peter had slept.

'If owt got into the yard, he'd be out there in a flash,' Wendy had said.

From the windowsill Theodore peered outside.

Michael's house was directly behind. He looked across into the back bedroom.

Philip was lying in bed. He was wearing his yellow trainers and his arm was laid over the duvet cover, his gold watch on his wrist. The duvet obscured his face.

Theodore glanced down at the yard below. Wendy Morris had shut the gate and was walking to the back door. She glanced up as she passed below.

Theodore jumped down onto the bed. On the bedside table he noticed a mug. He looked inside. There was an inch of greyish brown solidified hot chocolate in the bottom of the mug.

'Your dad never liked hot chocolate either,' Wendy had said to Laura.

It had been Wendy who had brought the mug of hot chocolate upstairs on the morning of the murder, thought Theodore, before he had discovered the body. She had sat on his bed and waited. She had sipped at her hot chocolate, knowing that her husband was not coming back up to bed; waiting for a reasonable hour to go downstairs and discover her husband's body. Then she would phone the police and let them know that someone had been in her yard in the night and killed her husband. But before she could call the police, Theodore had discovered the murder scene.

Downstairs he heard the back door being shut and then locked. A moment later there were heavy footsteps on the stairs.

He made for the landing at the top of the stairs but Wendy was already half way up. In her right hand she held her rolling pin. The rolling pin she had used to kill Arthur and finish off her husband...

Theodore raced down the stairs on the banister side, keeping to the wall.

As he passed, the rolling pin came down, sending a lump of plaster from the wall.

Reaching the bottom, he turned to see Wendy turning mid-flight, rolling pin in hand.

He made for the back door. It was closed. There was no cat flap. He carried on, into the downstairs bathroom. There was nowhere to hide. He ran back into the kitchen, but Wendy was blocking the door. He ran into the corner, by the sink. As far from Wendy as he could get.

Wendy stood in the middle of the kitchen, holding up the rolling pin. She slapped the rolling pin into the palm of her other hand. Then she did a few practice swipes, preparing herself to crack open the cat's skull.

Theodore backed as far back into the corner as he could. There was no escape.

Wendy raised her rolling pin. Theodore cowered. He closed his eyes, and braced himself for the blow. His end would be the same as Peter Morris's, he realized.

At least it would be over quickly. He braced himself and waited.

Then there was a sharp rapping on the window.

He opened his eyes, and looking up past Wendy, saw Irene's face pushed up against the kitchen window.

'You leave that cat alone!' Irene shouted through the glass.

A Nice Mug of Tea

'I'll make us a nice mug of tea,' Irene said, filling the kettle at the kitchen sink.

'I don't know what came over me,' Wendy said.

She was sitting at the kitchen table, wringing her hands.

'It's like he knew all along,' she said. 'He knew and he wasn't going to let it drop. He knew, I tell you.'

'He's just a cat,' Irene said, switching the kettle on, and then turning to her friend: 'An inquisitive one, I grant you that. But just a cat at the end of the day.'

Wendy shook her head. 'He was like a dog with the scent of a fox,' she said, glancing out of her kitchen window. 'He knew there was more to it… Than I was letting on.'

Irene tutted. 'It's all in your head,' she said.

'I'm going to call Fulford police station first thing in the morning. I'm going to tell the police everything. Come clean.'

'You're going to tell them you did it?'

'Me?' Wendy said, clucking her tongue. 'I didn't do it.'

She shook her head and clucked her tongue.

'But I know who did.'

'Who did it then?'

Irene leant forward.

'I heard everything,' Wendy said. 'Everything that went on that night… First it was that foreign girl. I heard them arguing… She hit him, but she didn't kill him. He was hurt all right. Lying there, groaning in pain. But I didn't go out to him… I sat there in the back bedroom and I waited.

'Then I heard a gate open and a minute later someone else came into the yard. There was a sharp crack and then Peter was quiet.

159

'I heard a gate scrape closed. Then it was quiet. Dead quiet. I sat there. I didn't go back to bed. I sat there, on his bed, and I waited.

'With the first light, I crept downstairs. I didn't go out. I made a cocoa in the dark and went back upstairs. I sat on his bed and waited… The funny thing was: I felt relief.'

'Relief?' Irene said.

'Yes, relief,' Wendy said. 'Relief it was over. Relief he was gone and never coming back.'

'I knew there was more to it,' Irene said, handing her a mug of tea. 'Than you were letting on…'

Wendy began to cry, big sobs from deep inside.

'Come on,' Irene said, putting a hand on Wendy's shoulder and patting her.

'You have no idea,' she spluttered. 'You have no idea what he was like.'

'I knew,' said Irene consolingly. 'I knew.'

'He cared more about his pigeons than me,' Wendy went on. 'For years I washed his socks and made his meals… and never any thanks. He even named his pigeons after girls he'd courted before me… Deirdre, Helen, Daisy, Ethel… I could hear him on a night, "Oh Ethel, you're such a pretty girl," or "Helen, I love you so much."'

'And then when Laura started seeing David he wouldn't even let me mention his name in the house. I thought maybe he would change his ideas when he knew Laura was serious about him. But when the baby came, he got even worse… He even went off his Jamaican Ginger Cake… Said it tasted foreign. Used to be his favourite as well.'

Irene shook her head and sighed.

'All those years I'd had to listen to him and nod my head and say "Yes, dear". Well, no more, I thought. Is that so bad?

'I sat there and waited. Then I heard that girl scream.'

'But if you didn't finish him off,' Irene said. 'Who did?'

Wendy sucked in a mouthful of air. 'It was him behind.'

She nodded to the kitchen window and the house behind.

'I don't know why he did it,' she went on. 'But the way I see it, he did me a favour. That's why I didn't say owt to them about it at the time…

'But that cat knew something was up. And he wouldn't let it lie.'

Theodore, sitting on the back wall, looked from Wendy's kitchen window to the house behind. He noticed the gate sitting on the concrete. He remembered Philip opening the gate to check if some sausage-stealing intruder was lurking on the other side. He remembered the gate scraping closed. Then he remembered Michael checking the soles of his trainers for blood on the morning of the murder.

The murderer always returned to the scene of the crime.

Greetings from Louisville

The picture of the back alley was complete. It was rich in detail. Theodore picked out Craig's house, where a cobblestone lay waiting to be discovered in the overgrown grass. He examined the back of his own house. The curtains in the back bedroom were closed, Emily still sleeping in bed.

Then there was Michael's own house. The curtains of the back bedroom were open a couple of inches. The dark silhouette of a figure behind the glass.

Theodore's eyes were then drawn to the house on the corner. He noted the pigeons, five of them, perched on the eaves. The door to the outbuilding was open and Peter Morris's slippered foot was visible, the concrete stained dark beneath.

In the centre of the picture, coming up the alley, was Arthur, a pigeon in his mouth, its head hanging to the side. Specks of blood dotted the cobblestones indicating where it had come from. It was all in the details, Theodore understood.

Michael gave the drawing its title, The Morning of the Murder, and signed it in the bottom right hand corner: Michael Butler.

Theodore should have known. The clues had been there all along, he realized.

Michael had finished off Peter Morris; then returned home. He had been unable to sleep. Had he left a bloody footprint behind at the murder scene? He checked his trainers. There was a faint smear of blood. He took them off his and washed them in the kitchen sink. He scrubbed at them frantically. Upstairs Philip slept on, unaware of what he'd done, or so he thought at the time.

Michael realized what he had to do. When the wife discovered her husband's body she would scream. He would be up, about to set off on an early morning run. He would dash in to see what was going on. He would trample over any evidence he might have left behind. He put on his running gear and waited.

Michael tended to go for a run in the late afternoon or early evening, Theodore realized. Even on the afternoon of York Races, he had left it until after the last race before setting off for his run. But on the morning following the murder, he had been kitted out ready for his run. That was the reason for him to be up and about at that early hour.

There was a tapping at Michael's front door. The bells of York Minster rang out seven o'clock.

Theodore's ears folded back. 'Me a model!' Emily had said laughing.

Emily was actually on time for once, Theodore realized.

Michael went to let her in.

A moment later, Theodore's eyes widened as he saw Emily enter the back living room. She was dressed in a pair of tight blue jeans and one of Jonathan's old checked shirts.

'You didn't forget our modelling date?' she said.

'How could I forget?' Michael said with a smile.

He indicated the purple chaise longue pushed up against the wall.

'How shabby chic,' Emily said, laughing nervously.

'Shall I get us a cup of tea before we start?' Michael said, walking into the kitchen and putting the kettle on; not waiting for a response.

Emily didn't sit down on the chaise longue straightaway. Instead she looked at some of the pictures on the walls. She paused in front of the picture of the back alley, not noticing the details. Then she examined the portrait of Philip, painted in acrylics. He stared lifelessly out from of the canvas.

'Is that supposed to be Philip?'

'Yes,' Michael said from the kitchen. 'Just a study I was working on.'

'I haven't seen him for a while...'

'No,' Michael said, the kettle reaching the boil. 'We're no longer an item, as they say.'

'Oh. I am sorry,' Emily said.

'Don't be,' Michael said from the kitchen.

She sat down on the chaise longue, her knees tightly together.

Theodore watched as she undid a button of Jonathan's shirt.

He looked to the kitchen, where Michael was crushing little white tablets with the back of a teaspoon. He spooned the white powder into Emily's cup of tea and stirred it in.

Michael put the two cups of tea onto the tray and carried it through into the living room. He placed the tray on a little side table beside the chaise longue. For the next few minutes the pair chatted.

'What type of tea is this?' Emily asked. 'It has a strange edge to it.'

'It's Yamamotoyama, said Michael.

'I don't think I've ever had that one before…'

She began to giggle.

'What did you say it's called again? Yamma… mamma.'

Michael laughed too. 'Yamamotoyama,' he said.

'Yammamammayammamamma…' said Emily, before collapsing into giggles.

Michael stood up and from behind the easel he picked up the little wooden mallet.

He glanced out of the kitchen window. He spotted Theodore eyeing him from within the ivy that hung over the wall.

'They will know my name,' he mouthed silently at the cat.

Theodore realized that Michael was intent on tidying up any loose ends.

He jumped down from the wall, then up onto the windowsill. It was a sash window. It was open at the top a couple of inches but not enough for him to get through. He peered through the glass into the room.

Emily was reclined on the chaise longue, another button on her shirt undone.

'So how would you like me?' she said, giggling. 'Is this all right?'

'I can always arrange you later,' said Michael and laughed.

Emily giggled. 'I like this tea,' she said, still giggling. 'It's very nice.'

'A nice cup of tea!' Michael said, clapping his hands together.

Emily reached over and took her cup of tea. 'Yammamamma…' she slurred, raising the cup to her lips.

'You drink it all up now,' Michael said, clutching the mallet behind the drawing board.

Theodore jumped up at the top of the window. He managed to get his paws into the gap. He pushed down and pushed himself forward as the window dropped under his weight. He landed in the middle of the room. He skidded to a halt between Emily and Michael.

'It's Theo!' Emily cried, clapping her hands together. 'It's my cat!'

Michael still had the small mallet in his hand, held behind the drawing board. Theodore dashed towards Emily, knocking the tea cup from her hand. It fell to the floor and smashed. The half-drunk tea spilled onto the parquet floor.

'Get out of here!' Michael shouted.

'Hey! Don't shout at my cat!'

'I'm allergic to cats!'

Theodore made it through the door into the hallway. He looked at the closed front door and then dashed up the stairs and into the back bedroom.

He jumped onto the double bed. The duvet fell away from Philip's face. A red pulp, with black scabs and shards of bone. It was more like a giant red lollipop that had been rolled in a grate of ashes than a human head.

Theodore looked at the body with the same expression as he would a dead moth.

Here we go again, he thought.

He had seen a dead human before. His instinct was to turn tail and run home. But Emily was downstairs and in no state to help.

The window over the bed was closed.

Behind him he heard footsteps pounding up the stairs. He dived under the bed.

'I know you're in there,' Michael said from the doorway.

Theodore positioned himself under the middle of the bed.

'I'm going to get you now,' he snarled.

He watched as Michael's face appeared at his own level, contorted into a grimace.

'I'm going to cut you in half and put you in formaldehyde.'

Theodore wasn't quite sure what formaldehyde was, having little interest in modern art. He edged backwards. He pushed up against something. It rolled away from him. He turned and inspected the object.

It was a wooden cylinder, about two feet long. A baseball bat. *Greetings from Louisville*, it said in cursive script down the side. He examined the end of the bat. It was caked in dried blood.

This is what Michael had used to finish Peter Morris off, realized Theodore, and then Philip. The murder weapon.

'Get out from there!' Michael hissed, his voice laced with anger. He swung his fist in a wide arc below the bed.

Theodore pressed himself into the corner. Just out of reach.

'Is everything all right up there?' Emily slurred from downstairs.

We are both for it now, thought Theodore.

'It's all right,' Michael said, 'I can manage. Just trying to get him out from under the bed.'

Michael approached the bottom of the bed. He yanked it away from the wall.

Theodore, exposed, dived back under the bed and out the other side. He ran through the door, before Michael could block him off, then back downstairs, past Emily, and into the kitchen.

'There,' Emily said. 'He's found his way out!'

Michael appeared at the top of the stairs, panting, the baseball bat held behind his back. 'I'm going to have to fumigate the house,' he said, coming back downstairs, breathing hard.

'I'm sorry,' Emily said.

Theodore miaowed at the back door.

'I'll let him out,' Emily said, making her way into the kitchen. 'I think it might be best if we both left.'

Theodore miaowed in agreement.

Emily tried the back door. It was locked. There was no key in the lock.

She turned and noticed the white powder smeared on the kitchen side.

'The door's locked,' Emily said slowly.

'I know,' said Michael.

Emily raised a hand to her temple. 'I feel very tired… after… all the… excitement,' she said. 'My head…'

She turned and fell to the floor.

Theodore watched from the corner, as Michael carried her back to the chaise longue and arranged her. Returning to his drawing board he picked up the meat tenderising mallet.

'Now we are going to see what cat brains look like!' Michael snarled, brandishing the mallet at Theodore.

Theodore ran past Michael, just avoiding a swipe from the mallet. He dashed into the hall and then back upstairs. This time, instead of making for the back bedroom, he ran into the front bedroom. There was a double bed. On top of one of the pillows there was a set of pink pyjamas, neatly folded.

The bedroom window was open, the sash pushed down. He jumped onto the bed and then up into the opening, balancing on the top of the window. The window dropped another inch under his weight.

He looked down. It was a twenty foot drop to the gravel forecourt below.

He looked up. There was the plastic gutter and then the eaves of the house.

He looked back and saw Michael standing in the doorway, clutching his mallet and grinning insanely.

He looked down once more.
Then jumped.

The Fine Art of Falling

Cats were designed to live in trees, so they know how to fall out of them.

They spread their legs out to increase their surface area and slow their fall. Their springy legs act as shock absorbers, cushioning the blow when they hit the ground. They rotate their bodies to make sure they land on their paws. Cats were designed to fall.

Throw a cow out of a window and it would be another story.

Theodore landed in the limestone gravel of Michael's forecourt. He looked back up at the window.

Michael stared down at him, his face red, his eyes wide.

Theodore exited through the open front gate and sprinted down the street and into the safety of the back alley.

His own house was empty. He paused in front of his empty food bowls. If Michael killed Emily, his bowls may never be filled again.

He would be destitute. A stray. Having to survive on a diet of rodents and whatever else he could catch.

He paced the kitchen floor, swishing his tail from side to side. He glanced at the clock on the kitchen wall. It was nearly eight o'clock. He wondered if Jonathan was on his way round. He entered the front room and looked out of the window and up the street. No Jonathan.

He paced the front room. Theodore didn't even know if Jonathan had arranged to come round that evening. But Jonathan was their only hope.

Theodore stared at his paws a moment.

Why couldn't Emily have dated a soldier, a professional wrestler, a bodyguard? Her only hope was a geologist...

He looked again at his empty food bowls.

There was no one else.

He would have to go and find him.

Jonathan was having his dinner when Theodore appeared at his kitchen window.

'Theodore!' he said, getting to his feet. 'What are you doing here?'

He opened the back door but Theodore did not enter the house. He jumped down onto the ground and miaowed at Jonathan.

Your girlfriend's been drugged by a psychopathic homicidal killer, he wanted to say.

'What is it, Theodore?' Jonathan said. 'How did you find me here?'

She's probably being cut up into little pieces by now.

'We didn't arrange anything for tonight,' Jonathan said, patting Theodore on the head.

If you don't come now, you're going to be looking for a new girlfriend...

'I'm in the middle of eating my dinner,' Jonathan said. 'I don't want it to get cold.'

Theodore made his way to the back gate, miaowing the whole time.

Jonathan returned to his pepperoni pizza. He bit into a slice and chewed. He could hear Theodore miaowing from his backyard. He got up and looked out of his kitchen window. Theodore was sitting on his back wall, staring back at him. When the cat saw him looking, it miaowed.

He reached for his mobile phone and called Emily's phone. She did not answer. He looked again out of his kitchen window at the grey cat.

A minute later Jonathan pushed the remains of his pizza into the kitchen bin and locked the back door behind him.

'This had better not be another dead cat in the allotments,' he said, as he shut his gate and followed Theodore's raised tail.

It might well be a dead girlfriend on the chaise longue, thought Theodore, as he trotted down the alley.

Back at No.17 Avondale Terrace, Jonathan discovered an empty house. There was Emily's mobile phone left on the arm of the sofa. There was one missed call. From him.

'She's probably just gone to the shops,' Jonathan said, following Theodore through to the kitchen.

He noticed Theodore's empty food bowls.

'So is that it?' he said. 'She went out without feeding you...'

Jonathan poured some biscuits into a bowl.

But Theodore turned his tailed up at them. He went over to the back door and miaowed.

Jonathan unlocked the door and followed Theodore out into the yard. The cat walked to the back gate. Jonathan noticed the back gate was unbolted. Perhaps Emily had gone out. If she had gone out of the back gate, she couldn't have gone far. He opened the gate and followed Theodore down the alley.

Theodore stopped in front of a back gate, opposite the house where Peter Morris had been killed. Reminded of the murder, Jonathan began to worry about his girlfriend. He stood in front of the gate.

Theodore looked up at him and then miaowed at the gate.

Jonathan hesitated. He didn't know who lived in this house. Emily had not mentioned being friends with anyone on the street. She kept herself to herself; more so after the murder of her neighbour.

'Are you sure about this?' he said to Theodore.

The cat miaowed back at him. *Just get a move on.*

'You'd better be.'

Suddenly Diane appeared out of nowhere.

'I want a word with you,' she said, prodding her forefinger at his chest.

'Now's not a good time,' Jonathan said. 'I'm a bit busy.'

'I want to know about my cat,' Diane said. 'You didn't bury him in your garden, did you?'

'No,' Jonathan said. 'Not exactly.'

'I didn't think so.'

'I was going to,' Jonathan said. 'But then I threw him in a wheelie bin.'

'You did what?'

'Look, does it really matter now? He was dead. It was a little white lie.'

'You put my cat in a wheelie bin!' Diane screamed.

A piece of chewing gum dropped from her mouth onto the ground.

Jonathan took a step backwards.

'A little white lie!'

'It's a long story and I really don't have time to tell it now.'

'You threw my Arthur into a wheelie bin?' Diane screamed. 'You heartless arsehole!'

She pushed Jonathan in the chest with her fingers.

'I have to go,' Jonathan said, but Diane was blocking his path, her face in his.

He tried to step round her but she moved too, her fingers poking at his chest.

Craig Foster had been watching the altercation from the window of his attic room. He rushed downstairs and out into the back alley.

'What's going on?' he gasped. 'Are you all right?'

Diane turned to face him. 'What's it to you?' she said. 'You ginger nutter.'

'I saw you arguing,' Craig panted. 'I came to help.'

'I don't need any help from you,' Diane barked.

Craig's face dropped. 'But…'

'But what? How are you going to help? Are you going to bring my cat back? Are you going to bring my husband back? Well?'

'Well, no,' Craig said.

'I really need to get going,' Jonathan interrupted.

'You're not going anywhere,' Diane said. 'Not until you tell me why you dropped my cat in a wheelie bin.'

'Look, now's not a good time,' Jonathan said and barged past her.

'You haven't heard the last of this,' Diane screamed after him.

Jonathan carried on down the hill, not looking round. Then Theodore emerged from his hiding place beneath a hedge and trotted after him.

Craig stood next to Diane and watched them go, tears in his eyes. 'I came to help,' he blubbed.

'Well, you weren't much help, were you?' Diane said.

She began to walk back to her house.

'He hasn't heard the last of it,' she called out.

Jonathan and Theodore exited the alley onto Avondale Terrace and then counted the houses back up the hill. He stopped in front of No.7. The front door was painted glossy black with a shiny brass knocker. He knocked on the door. He waited. He knocked again. Finally the door opened a couple of inches.

'This might sound stupid,' Jonathan said into the gap, 'but is my girlfriend here?'

'Your girlfriend?' Michael said.

'Yes. Emily Blenkin. She lives up the street.'

There was a pause, and then Michael said, 'Yes. Emily's modelling for me...'

'Modelling?' Jonathan said. 'She didn't mention it... I was worried.'

'I am working on her portrait,' Michael said. 'Didn't she say?'

Through the gap in the door, Jonathan noticed that Michael was indeed holding a pencil.

'I didn't know,' Jonathan said. 'She didn't say anything about modelling.'

'Yes, modelling,' Michael said. 'I'll get back to it if there's nothing else. Wouldn't want to lose the flow, you know.'

From behind Jonathan, Theodore miaowed.

Michael was about to close the door.

'I need to speak to her a minute,' Jonathan said. 'It's important. It's about her cat...'

'I'm afraid you can't at the moment,' Michael said.

'Excuse me?'

'She fell asleep,' Michael explained.

'Asleep? But I really need to speak to her.'

Jonathan moved towards the front door.

'You can come in a minute,' Michael said, 'but she's fast asleep I tell you…'

Theodore watched as Jonathan entered Michael's house and the door was shut behind him. He raced back into the alley and returned to the boundary wall of Michael's house. Inside, he saw Jonathan enter the lounge. Emily was laid out provocatively on the chaise longue. He looked at the parquet floor. The broken tea cup and its contents had been cleared away and cleaned up.

Jonathan put his hand on Emily's shoulder.

'Emily,' he said, shaking her. 'You need to wake up.'

Michael returned to his drawing board and picked up the little wooden mallet.

Theodore dropped down to the ground and then jumped up onto the windowsill. The sash window had been closed.

'She must have relapsed,' Jonathan said.

'Relapsed?' Michael said, clutching the mallet behind the drawing board.

'Yes,' Jonathan said. 'She's hypersensitive to certain foods…'

'I didn't know,' Michael said.

'Chinese food, in particular.'

'I did make her a cup of green tea,' Michael said.

'That might have done it,' Jonathan said, bending over his girlfriend.

Michael approached, the mallet raised over Jonathan's head. Ready to strike.

Theodore miaowed through the glass as loudly as he could.

Jonathan looked round and saw Theodore on the windowsill. He turned and saw Michael, a wooden mallet in his hand.

'What's that?' Jonathan said, squaring up to Michael.

'It's a mallet,' Michael said. 'You know for tenderising steaks.'

'But what are you doing with it?'

Michael hesitated.

Jonathan glanced back at his prone girlfriend, then back to Michael.

'Well?'

'I use it,' Michael said. 'As a rest. You know, so I don't smudge my work.'

'Well,' Jonathan said, turning back to Emily, 'I think I'd better get her home.'

Jonathan lifted her up from the chaise longue and placed her over his shoulder in a fireman's lift.

As he shut the front door behind him, he murmured into Emily's ear, 'Let's get you home…'

They Will Know My Name

Cats have a killer instinct, though their owners prefer to gloss over the fact.

The instinct in most humans is hidden well below the surface, smothered by thousands of years of civilisation. Not many humans have the desire or even the potential to kill these days, Theodore realized. Especially not another human being.

Michael was an exception. He had killed Peter Morris. He had killed his partner Philip. He was about to kill Emily. He was a killer.

Jonathan put Emily to bed. Theodore settled by her side and reassured himself that she was going to be fine.

In her drug-induced sleep, he heard her say: 'I don't want to model for you anymore.'

Downstairs Jonathan watched television. He had opened a bottle of red wine and had found a Swedish crime drama on the television.

When he saw Theodore enter the front room, he said, 'Looks like it's me and you tonight.'

Theodore sat on his lap but couldn't settle.

'That guy gave me the creeps,' Jonathan said to Theodore.

Theodore purred in agreement.

'Lucky you warned me about the mallet.'

Jonathan took a large drink from his glass of wine.

Then there was a knock at the door.

Theodore followed Jonathan.

There were two police officers.

'Are you Jonathan?' one of them said. 'Jonathan Fielder?'

'Yes,' said Jonathan.

'Do you know a Diane Banks?'

'Diane?' Jonathan said. 'I know someone called Diane.'

'Did you have an altercation with her this evening? In the alley behind?'

'An altercation? Not really. She was upset and I tried to get past her.'

'Did you push her?'

'She was in my way.'

'Did you push her?'

'I pushed past her.'

'So you pushed her.'

'I suppose I did. But she pushed me first.'

'She says that you threw her dead cat into a wheelie bin.'

'Yes. I did. It's a long story, but I didn't know it was hers. I found it and brought it back here.'

'I think you are going to have to come with us and make a statement. She is quite upset about it all.'

'Really? Now? Can't it wait until morning. My girlfriend is upstairs asleep.'

'I'm sure she'll still be here when you get back,' a police officer quipped.

'I think it best if you come with us now,' the other said. 'These are quite serious allegations against you.'

Jonathan shook his head. 'I'll get my jacket,' he said.

Theodore watched from the front window as Jonathan got into the back of the police van, which had stopped in the middle of the street. After a minute or two the van pulled away.

He went upstairs and checked on Emily. She was fast asleep. He dabbed at her face but she didn't wake.

As the light began to fade and the air grew cold, Theodore took up position in the ivy that grew over the boundary wall of Michael's house. Michael was doing the washing up in the kitchen. When he brought his kitchen bin out and emptied it into the bin in the yard, he spotted Theodore.

'So you want to know why?' he asked.

'Well, I could tell you how he muttered "Your sort disgusts me," as I was putting my rubbish out one night,' Michael said. 'I could tell you how he drove a wedge between mother and daughter because of his racist views… Yes. I had an eye on the old bigot for years. I was doing the world a favour.'

Theodore stared into Michael's eyes imploringly.

'And what about Philip?' he wanted to say.

'Philip suspected that I'd done it but he didn't know for sure.'

Theodore continued staring down at Michael.

'He began making demands… A new pair of trainers, an expensive watch, a meal out. It all adds up… I'm a struggling artist, you know. I don't have that sort of money. I had to deal with him before he said something. It was his own fault really.'

Theodore's eyes widened further.

'And Emily? Well, I was getting into the swing of it… Get it? The swing of it!'

Michael mimicked swinging a baseball bat, a sick grin on his face.

'Then I have my reputation to think about,' he went on. 'One day my pictures will be priceless. Once people know the background…'

He replaced the cover to the metal bin with a clatter. 'It's a pity I don't do pets…' he said, still grinning.

He turned to go back inside but paused.

Then he turned back to Theodore. 'So, now you know the truth, what are you going to do about it, little pussy cat?'

Theodore considered attempting a feline arrest but knew it would be futile.

Michael said, 'Nothing. There's nothing you can do about it.'

Theodore wanted to say that there was just one more thing, as he had heard his hero Lieutenant Columbo quip before delivering the killer line and nailing the criminal. But he did not say anything. He was just a cat after all.

'Well, if there's nothing else,' Michael said. 'I need to get on. I'm going down to London tomorrow.'

He turned and went back into his house, shutting the door behind him.

In the kitchen Michael took his mobile phone from his pocket and made a call.

'Henry?' he said. 'It's Michael... You know, Mikey from Yorkshire... Yes, I know it's late... But I'm coming down to London tomorrow... I've got something for you.'

He paused, listening to Henry talk.

'I know the last pictures didn't sell well,' he said. Then: 'These will make my name... I can promise you that. They will be priceless one day... I just need a bit of an advance on them. That's all.'

He paced the kitchen, his mobile held tightly to his ear, his pink head glistening beneath the fluorescent kitchen light.

'Look. I'll see you tomorrow. You won't be disappointed. Not when I tell you the story behind them...'

He finished the phone call before Henry could protest. Then, from on top of a cupboard, he got down a brown suitcase. He began taking his pictures down from the walls and putting them into the suitcase.

Once his suitcase was packed, Michael returned to the kitchen and from a cupboard he took a handheld electric circular saw he had bought that morning from B&Q and went upstairs.

Moments later the bathroom light was turned on.

Theodore heard both bath taps turned on and water began to run from the bottom of a pipe into the drain. From the bathroom there came a whirring, and then the whine as metal cut bone.

Water gushed into the drain, through the round metal grate. Theodore watched as the water turned red.

Froth formed on the drain grate.

Theodore looked up at the bathroom window and the shadows dancing behind the mottled glass.

Bin Day

The dim hour before dawn is a magical time, if you are a cat. The birds are awake. Most cats are awake. Most people are asleep. Michael, however, was wide awake.

The night before bin day, people put their bin bags against their back walls. As the access into the back alley is too tight for the bin lorry to enter, a man gathers all the bags and stacks them in a big pile against the side of Wendy Morris's house. The lorry parks next to the access to the alley and the bin men heft the bags into the back of the bin lorry.

Michael waited until first light before putting out his rubbish. He had placed his bags in a neat row at the base of Wendy's wall. Now he stood in front of his bedroom window and waited.

Another person was also up early that morning. In her mauve dressing gown and fur-lined slippers, Wendy Morris paced her kitchen, glancing now and again at the telephone on the side and then to the clock on the wall. Waiting for a reasonable hour to call the police. She put the kettle on and made herself a cocoa.

Theodore lay on the pillow beside Emily. His ears twitched as he listened to the early morning noises from outside. His thoughts flicked back to the evening before. He remembered the red water that had gushed out into the drain, leaving pink and yellow scum over the grate.

There was no way he could prove that Michael had killed Peter Morris, but perhaps he could get him for Philip's murder.

Theodore got to his paws and jumped down onto the floor. He crossed to the window and, standing up on his hind legs, poked his head up behind the closed curtains.

Against Wendy's wall there was a line of three full bin liners, each closed at the top with parcel tape. He knew they did not belong to Wendy. Her bin bags were further up the wall of her house, nearer the street. He watched as a bin man added a dozen more bags to the bottom of the wall. No doubt the three ominous black bags would soon be beneath a mountain of rubbish, Theodore realized. His thoughts returned to the dancing silhouette behind the bathroom window.

He returned to his pillow and tried to wake Emily, dabbing at her face with the pads of his paws, but she was sound asleep, her mouth open. Jonathan had yet to return from Fulford Police Station. He was by himself, he realized.

In the grey light, he padded down the stairs and made for the cat flap.

From the back wall, he glanced up at Michael's bedroom window. The curtains were open; a dark silhouette behind the glass. He saw the bin man further up the hill, half a dozen bin bags in each hand, carrying them to the bottom to add to the ones already piled up against Wendy's wall; he whistled as he worked. He threw the bags onto the pile and then returned up the hill to gather more.

Theodore peered into Wendy's kitchen. Wendy was sitting at the kitchen table, the telephone in front of her, a mug of cocoa in her hand. Every minute or so she glanced at the clock on the wall.

The bin man was halfway up the hill, his back to Theodore. Theodore jumped down into the alley and dashed across to the bin bags piled up against Wendy's wall.

He slid a claw across the tight shiny black surface. The bag split open to reveal a second shiny black surface. Double-bagged!

He heard footsteps approach the corner. He swiped at the black shiny plastic again.

'Get out of it,' the bin man shouted, stamping his feet theatrically at the cat.

Theodore turned and dashed past the bin man, side stepping him, then raced back up the hill.

Back upstairs in the bedroom, Emily was still asleep. Theodore stood up behind the curtain once more. The three bin liners were now hidden by the ever growing pile of rubbish. In the distance he heard the bin lorry approach. The bin man who had seen Theodore off stood waiting beside the mountain of rubbish for his colleagues to join him.

An orange light began to flash against the side of Wendy's house, and soon two other men entered the back alley and began shifting the bin bags, tossing them into the back of the waiting lorry. Finally they got to the bottom of the pile.

A bin man picked up the last bag and began to carry it out into the street.

'You've lost something,' one of his colleagues shouted back at him.

On the ground lay a fingerless hand and forearm, wrapped in cling film. On the wrist there was a gold Rolex.

Theodore watched as one of the bin men shook his bald head slowly from side to side. 'Now I've seen it all,' he said.

The bin man took out his mobile phone and called the police.

At the same time Wendy took a last sip of cocoa, put down her mug; then picked up her phone and dialled 999.

The alarm clock went off. Emily rolled over and snoozed it. 'Too early,' she mumbled sleepily.

Theodore walked past the bed and into the front bedroom. He jumped up onto the table in front of the window. From down the street, he heard a door open and then close.

In the distance he heard a police siren.

Michael walked to the pavement and placed his suitcase by the kerb. He glanced at his watch. He took out his mobile phone. Sweat beaded on his pink forehead.

Then a taxi appeared at the bottom of the hill. It pulled up against the kerb. He read the insignia on the side: Crow Line Taxis.

Ahmet swung open the taxi door and got out to help his first customer of the day with his luggage.

'Morning,' he said to Michael, recognising him as the artistic type who lived several doors down the hill from his own house.

Michael already had his suitcase in his hand as Ahmet approached.

'I can manage,' he said abruptly.

Ahmet opened the boot and Michael pushed the suitcase inside.

'I'm in a hurry,' Michael said, getting into the back of the taxi.

Ahmet closed the boot and got into the driving seat.

Michael looked out of the car window.

He saw the large grey cat staring down at him from a window. The cat blinked at him. He waved goodbye to the cat and mouthed, 'Bye, bye Pussy Cat.'

The sirens grew louder.

Theodore jumped down from the windowsill and headed downstairs.

'You know, I live on this street,' Ahmet said, getting in the driver's seat. 'Just up there... First customer of the morning and it's one of my neighbours. What a coincidence!'

'The station,' Michael said. 'I'm going to the railway station.'

'Business or pleasure?' Ahmet said, putting the car into gear.

He pulled the car into the middle of the road, between the lines of parked cars.

'Just drive,' Michael said. 'I'm not in the mood for small talk.'

Ahmet drove up the hill, not shifting up from second gear. As they neared the top of the road, a police car turned in, preventing them from exiting. Ahmet began to reverse into a gap in the parked cars to allow the police car to pass.

'Keep going!' Michael shouted. 'I have a train to catch.'

Ahmet glanced back down the street and saw another police car begin to ascend the hill, its siren turned on. He glanced at the police car in front, its siren now turned on. He glanced at his backseat passenger, his face red and dripping sweat.

'You're going to miss your train,' Ahmet said. He put the handbrake on and took the key from the ignition. Then he stepped out of his taxi and locked the doors.

The police car stopped in front and two officers got out.

Michael slapped his hands uselessly against the car window.

'Let me out!' he screamed from behind the glass.

'What seems to be the problem here?' one of the officers asked Ahmet.

'This gentleman appears to be in a rush this morning,' Ahmet said. 'With all the sirens, I thought I'd better stop.'

'We'd better have a word with him,' a police officer said. 'If you could unlock the doors…'

Ahmet clicked his car key and the passenger door swung open, across the pavement.

Michael jumped out of the taxi and faced the police officer.

'In a hurry?' the police officer said.

'Yes,' Michael said, and turned and began to run down the street.

As he passed the access into the back alley, he spotted the grey fluffy cat crouching against the wall.

And Theodore spotted the red-faced Michael as he flashed past. He saw Irene and Rocky crossing the road at the bottom of the hill, Rocky straining on his lead; out for his early morning walk.

Theodore dashed out onto the pavement, turned and caught the German shepherd's eye. Then he ran up the hill.

Rocky broke free of his lead and bolted up the hill after the big grey cat. Unfortunately Michael was in his way.

Michael's legs were taken out by the German shepherd. He was sent sprawling onto the pavement. Within seconds police officers were over him, one of them with his knee on his back.

'I think you've got some explaining to do,' he said, cuffing him.

Theodore watched from the forecourt of a house as Michael was dragged to his feet and walked towards a police car. Rocky was trotting up and down the street, his tongue lolling, while Irene called for him, 'Get here now!'

Theodore watched as Michael was put in the back of a police car. More police cars and vans had arrived; their sirens blaring out a symphony.

Later the police would discover Philip's dismembered body in the bin bags in the back alley. Later, his bashed-in head would be fished out of the muddy waters of the Ouse, tied up in a Waitrose bag for life.

His fingers and teeth would never be recovered.

Poppycock!

'Clementhorpe Killer Caught!' the headline in *The Press* shouted the next day from Wendy's kitchen table.

Wendy was sitting at the table with Irene.

'Well, at least you can move on now,' Irene said.

'Aye suppose so,' Wendy said. 'Talking of moving on, I saw a For Sale sign outside Diane's. Reckon she's moving back to Lancashire.'

'It'll be bought and let out like the rest of them.'

'Craig Foster's house too. He must have decided to move on too.'

'Investors,' Irene muttered. 'They'll soon snap them up. They keep putting leaflets through my door. Can't wait for me to pop my clogs.'

'You've got a good few years left in you,' Wendy said.

'I've got my dog to look after,' Irene said. 'I have to keep going for him.'

Irene opened the paper and began to flick through the other stories.

'Look at this,' she said. 'The Lucky Twin takeaway has been closed down.'

'Why's that then?'

'They've been done by Trading Standards for spicing up their food with opiates.'

'I don't believe that for a minute,' Wendy said. 'Sounds like a lot of poppycock!'

She slapped the table and laughed.

Irene laughed too and Wendy laughed even harder.

After Irene had left, Wendy had another visitor.

Her daughter pushed her pram through into the kitchen. On top of the pram was wedged a cat carrier.

186

'What's that you've got in there?' Wendy asked.

'What do you think it is? It's a kitten,' Laura said. 'It's for you.'

'But I don't like cats,' Wendy said. 'You know that.'

'Dad never liked cats,' Laura said. 'But that doesn't mean that you can't like them.'

Wendy shook her head.

'It'll keep you company,' Laura said. 'Go on.'

'You'd better get him out so I can have a look at him.'

Laura parked the pram in the backyard and made herself a coffee, the kitten purring on Wendy's lap the whole time.

They sat at the kitchen table.

'Joseph will be waking shortly,' Laura said, 'and I don't have any food with me.'

'I'm sure I've got something here you could give him. Porridge oats. I could make up some porridge for him.'

At that moment Joseph began to cry.

'I should really get going,' Laura said. 'But I'll call round tomorrow to see how you and the kitten are getting on.'

She turned to her mother: 'Best to let bygones be bygones.'

'Aye,' Wendy said. 'Best to let sleeping dogs lie.'

Later, Theodore watched as the kitten kneaded Wendy's stomach, purring loudly. It was a tortoiseshell: a mishmash of colours: white, marmalade, grey and black. Wendy stroked the kitten as she watched her soap opera. 'I'll call you Splodge,' she said.

Theodore got to his paws and stretched. Before returning home, he paid a visit to Zeynep and Ahmet's. From inside the house, the new baby cried.

Ahmet was standing over the Moses basket.

'You can pick him up, you know,' Zeynep said.

'I'm afraid to,' Ahmet said, peering down at the pink shrivelled baby with bruised eyes. 'He's so small.'

'It'll be fine,' Zeynep said. 'Just don't drop him!'

Ahmet picked the baby up and held him to his chest. He thought of the dolls' house he had made for the baby. The little house that Zeynep had smashed up.

'I will make him a railway set,' Ahmet said. 'For when he is bigger. It will have tunnels and bridges, and a station and station master...'

'You can make it in your shed,' Zeynep said and smiled.

From the back bedroom window Bal and Belle peered out. They would soon be removed from the bedroom which would become a nursery. They blinked hello at Theodore.

Theodore blinked back.

He understood that Bal had been the key to unlocking the mystery. The Lucky Twin had held the key. Zeynep had hit Peter Morris over the head but had not killed him. She believed she had taken a man's life but she had actually brought life into this world.

Theodore closed his eyes.

Who was ultimately responsible for killing Peter Morris?

Zeynep had hit him with the cobblestone. Wendy had ignored his cries for help. Then Michael had finished him off with his baseball bat, a Souvenir from Louisville, wherever that might be.

But if Peter Morris had not made the racist remark to Zeynep, he might still be alive. If he had been a little nicer to his wife, Wendy, he might still be alive. If he had not insulted Michael, he might still be alive. So, in a way, Peter Morris had been responsible for his own ending.

He just hadn't reckoned on having a psychopathic killer living behind, and who does?

Michael Butler had stored up his grievances inside. He had wanted fame and fortune for his art but they had not been forthcoming. He had spent his hours dwelling on the unfairness of life. Hatred for his fellow man festered inside with no outlet. Now, in a high security prison, he would get the therapy he needed through his art. He would produce masterworks which would never be seen outside Her Majesty's Prisons.

Then Theodore realised that he had been blinded by his own first impressions of Michael to make him a serious suspect in his investigation; his own prejudice had shielded Michael. If

Theodore had acted sooner, he might have put an end to Michael's murderous ways before he had killed Philip.

Dried leaves blew down the back alley.

Theodore wandered restlessly home.

Jonathan and Emily were in the front room.

'To think I modelled for him!' Emily said.

'I think you had a narrow escape,' Jonathan said, putting the newspaper down. 'We both did.'

'Don't you mean all three of us?' Emily said, nodding and smiling at Theodore, now standing in the middle of the room.

'Yes,' Jonathan said. 'I'm not sure what would have happened the other night if he hadn't turned up.'

The telephone in the corner began ringing.

'It'll be my mother,' said Emily.

They let it go to the answerphone.

'I can't believe it was the man from down the hill who did it,' Emily's mother said into the machine. 'I heard on the news that he's homosexual too. Well, I never thought you could get homicidal homosexuals!'

Emily snatched up the telephone. 'What about Ted Bundy?' she said.

'Pardon?' her mother said, surprised that the telephone had been answered. 'Who's this Ted Bundy?'

'He was a gay serial killer,' Emily said. 'Targeted young men. He used to dress up as a clown too.'

'Did he now?' her mother said. 'Well, I guess it takes all sorts.'

'Yes, Mum,' Emily said. 'I guess it does.'

'Don't they say: it's always the ones you don't suspect?'

'They do indeed.'

After Emily had finished speaking to her mum and had said hello to her dad, she turned to Jonathan.

'After everything that's happened here,' she said, 'I think it might be an idea to move. After everything that's happened, I don't think I'm ever going to be comfortable round here again.'

'What do you mean move?' Jonathan said. 'When were you going to tell me?'

'Well, I'm asking?'

'Asking?'

'Asking if you'd like to move in together. With me and Theodore. It makes sense. We need somewhere bigger… You're paying rent for your place and spending half the time round here anyway. It just makes sense.

'And I'm sure Theodore would love a garden. He might not get into such mischief if he had a garden to play in.'

'So, you think we should all move in together and play happy families?'

'Why not?' Emily said, chewing on her thumbnail. 'What do you say?'

'Sounds like a plan,' Jonathan said. 'Where were you thinking?'

'I think a different area,' Emily said. 'After everything that's happened in Clementhorpe, I think we should move somewhere different.'

'Like where?'

'How about Acomb?'

'I'm sure you get more for your money in Acomb,' Jonathan said.

'It's a bit suburban but perhaps the suburban life is better than having your neighbours knocked off.'

'Let's do it then,' Jonathan said.

'Yes, let's,' Emily said.

Jonathan bent towards Emily and, as they kissed, Theodore slunk outside.

He sat on the back wall as the sun sank behind South Bank. He gazed over at the brick walls of the alleys and houses. Further up the hill they had begun to lay tarmac over the cobbles, the black blanket covering over a hundred years of history. Further down the hill a street lamp bathed the remaining blue cobblestones in golden light.

Theodore knew that it would soon be gone. He sensed the massive change that was to come. He did not know the specifics, but he understood that everything familiar was about to change. The back alley would be gone. The people he knew on the street would be gone. He would be yanked out of this world and plonked down in another. A world of suburbia and gardens, and new neighbours…

But Theodore liked it here. He liked the alley. He liked napping in the front window in the afternoon sunshine. He liked Clementhorpe. He didn't want to move to Acomb. Whatever Acomb might entail.

He raised his head and began a low mewling, becoming higher pitched before breaking into full wail.

He sang his lament to the cobbles of the back alleys; the weathered bricks that made up the walls; the worn slate roof tiles; the satellite dishes perched under eaves pointing south; the old ladies nattering over tea and biscuits; the men busy in their sheds or jogging up and down the street; the cats sleeping under hedges or basking in the sun on flat felt roofs; the dogs whining for walks in backyards; the pigeons gathered on the ridges; the black and white geese flying over, en route to Rowntree Park, the solitary magpie perched on a television aerial…

He sang his song: his farewell to Clementhorpe: his home.

Windows up and down the street were abruptly pulled shut. As everyone knows, the singing of cats is not to everybody's taste.

May 2012 – December 2016, York